AF427126

John Houlihan is a novelist and short story writer publishing books including The Seraph Chronicles and Mon Dieu Cthulhu! series, *The Cricket Dictionary* and the BSFA-award nominated The *Constellation of Alarion*. He has also appeared in numerous sci-fi and fantasy short story collections including Signals, Near Future Fictions, When Shadows Creep, Corridors, Forgotten Sidekicks, Musketeers vs Cthulhu and many more.

He currently works for Modiphius Entertainment as an ENNIE-award winning game designer, creative lead and narrative director and works for many other TTRPG companies including Wizards of the Coast, Need Games and Monolith. He was also editor-in-chief of *Dragon+*. Before that he was a journalist and broadcaster for over thirty years, working in news, sport and especially videogames. He worked for *The Times*, *Sunday Times* and *Cricinfo* and is the former editor-in-chief of *Computer and Video Games.com*. He still works as a video game consultant and script writer.

Away from the written word he has an unnatural fondness for cricket, football, snowboarding, cycling, music, playing guitar and all forms of sci-fi, fantasy and horror. He has an unnatural dread about writing about himself in the third person and currently lives in his home town of Watford in the UK, because, well frankly, someone has to.

Find him at www.john-houlihan.net and @johnh259 on X.com

CONTENTS

THE SERAPH CHRONICLES BOOK THREE:

TOMB OF THE AEONS

CHAPTER ONE:
THE GREAT WASTE

At first the great dunes seem as unchanging as the aeons, yet one soon learns they are not fixed things, but as mutable and storm-ridden as the ocean. The sands constantly shift, reforming and remaking themselves under the influence of the wind and the baleful gaze of the sun, so that one is always looking at a frozen moment in perpetual chaos.

A difficult thing at first for a simple panzer commander to understand and so different from what we had experienced just the year before. Then, the dappled green forests, meadows and lush farmland had been our autobahn, as France fell in little over a month, yielding to a combination of armoured Blitzkrieg and her own complacency.

Here the heat parches, burns, withering mind and flesh and we are steel ships sailing over a barren ocean. The Arabs say water is life itself, but here fuel, fuel is even more precious, the lifeblood of our panzers, the only means to seek sanctuary from the relentless boiling fury above.

Forgive me, I ramble, but I have seen such things this night, terrible things, things that no sane mind should have to witness and now I struggle to find meaning, struggle to retain my precarious grip on sanity. Before the war I was a poet and used to have all the words I ever needed, but the Fatherland has no use for poets any more, only killers.

You say I am a prisoner of war now and I believe and accept it gentlemen, but forgive me, this is not how one should begin a proper military report. Let me start again from the very beginning. Forgive any minor lapses in my poor English, but I will try to order my thoughts as best I can, so that you may understand how it all came to pass. Then you may judge the degree of my sanity …or its lack, for yourself.

It is March 1941 and after our triumphs of the previous year, the war enters a new phase and is being fought on a new front, the desert wastes of North Africa. During *Weihnachten* or Christmas of the previous year, the British had chased our unfortunate Italian allies all the way back into Libya sending them packing with their tails between their legs, destroying and capturing an entire army group. Following this humiliation, it was decided to reinforce the front and we, veterans of the Third Panzers, were dispatched to shore up the leaky Italian defences. We were given a new mission and a new name, the 5th Light Division, or as history will always know us from that moment onwards, the *Afrika Korps*.

Our journey began inauspiciously, for those who believe in such things, for just before we embarked from Naples the transport *Leverkusen* caught fire at anchor, spilling men and armour into the ocean and we lost a number of our force before a single shot had been fired. Nor was the crossing the smoothest of journeys. The Mediterranean was unseasonably choppy, British warplanes from Malta harried and harassed our convoy and our travelling companions, a unit of SS with a strange radial-flashed insignia, made my men distinctly uneasy.

Yet by February we had finally landed at Tripoli and felt the heat and dust of the dark continent for the first time. It was stifling and oppressive but we were willing, eager, to test ourselves against the British and their colonial allies. For we had a new commander too, Generalleutnant Erwin Rommel formerly of the 7th panzers, a bold and daring leader who the men are already calling *Der Wüstenfuchs* – the Desert Fox.

I believe our original orders were simply to hold the line, but the Desert Fox is a hunter, a formidable predator and we immediately went on the offensive, bursting out from El Agheila, giving you British, how you say, 'a bloody nose' and putting you in full flight back towards the Egyptian border. I heard on the radio that a small pocket of resistance was still holding out at Tobruk but we were part of the vanguard and had already pushed far beyond that, at the forefront of Rommel's great right hook which outflanked your valiant Tommies.

Oh, but these are the finest of days to be a panzer soldier, your tracks roll across the open desert, driver, gunner and loader working in perfect harmony as you designate the target, engage the enemy and watch as they 'brew up' – as I believe you say – one by one. There is a poetry, something glorious to it at the time, though afterwards, when one sees the broken metal and charred, twisted bodies, one is reminded of both the true cost of war and how transitory notions of honour are.

The day had been long and hard, but we had emerged victorious from a prolonged engagement with a squadron of your British Crusaders and Matildas. I counted four which had fallen directly beneath the 75 millimetre of '*Ingrid*' our Mark IV panzer and as dusk began to fall, we should have been well satisfied with our day's work. The smoking hulls of both British tanks and our own panzers littered the plain but as the British retreat became a rout, I was determined to add to our tally. With the last light failing, we pursued a lone Matilda Mark II decked with command pennons into the deeper wastes.

Perhaps I was guilty of chasing glory, perhaps it was simple blood lust which consumed me, a *jaeger's* instinct to pursue, but ignoring my crew's unspoken wishes, I drove them on, pushing them harder as we moved and fired, trying to hit the enemy tank. Foolishness, madness, blindness, I was guilty of all three, but as the first stars began to peep out from the heavens, a well directed shell caught the Matilda's rear tracks and it shuddered, shedding steel and metal.

"Halt." I commanded over the intercom and Jürgen, our driver, locked both tracks bringing *Ingrid* to a standstill. "Give the Tommies the opportunity to bail out – once they are clear, put an armour piercing round through the hull. We will take the survivors back for questioning but wait for my order."

"*Jawohl,* Herr Oberleutnant."

Quickly I popped the turret hatch and scanned the Matilda with my binoculars for signs of the crew leaping clear. None emerged and just as my impatience was on the point of getting the better of me, the enemy vehicle exploded, gouts of flame erupting from its hatches, flaring into the dusk. Our shell must have penetrated deeper than it had first appeared, perhaps catching the engine or the fuel tanks. I sighed, my ire expended, but this is war and one cannot mourn too deeply for one enemy tank crew's demise. One scarcely has time to mourn one's own dead.

I began to hunker down, pulling the hatch behind me and gave the order to move again when a sound caught my attention and there, not fifty metres away, came a British heavy Crusader rumbling over the top of the dune. It must have been paralleling our course, damn my eagerness! Now it had us cold in its sights. The Crusader came to a halt and I was shouting, "*Vorwärts! Ziel wieder links*! Move! Target left, target left!" desperately. Our tracks bit feebly into the sand and our own turret began to turn, but slowly, far too slowly and then the Crusader's barrel belched a great gout of flame and there was no time for thought any more.

The tugging on my shoulder was gentle at first and I mumbled 'leave me Ilse I must sleep some more' and tried to roll away from it. But quickly it became more insistent and now my wife was shaking me and I groaned, feeling a pain that seemed to have no place in that gentle Bavarian spring. My eyes opened the smallest portion into semi-darkness but it was not the face of my Ilse which greeted me, but the rough, bearded features of Kurt, my radio operator and second-in-command. The memory of the Crusader's muzzle flash came back in a rush and quickly I sat up. Pain lanced through my head and I would have howled, but instead confined myself to a lingering groan.

"Ah, so you're alive, Herr Oberleutnant. *Gut*."

"Barely it seems. Report."

"It is not good, Dieter and Otto are dead, for a while we thought you were too. *Ingrid* is *tot*, the shell blew half her turret off. The British must have thought they had killed us all and they didn't stop to check. Jürgen's wounded but not badly. Oh, and Little Hans, Dieter's cat, survived as well."

I opened my eyes momentarily and was not best pleased with the results as the pain grew more intense. Kurt pressed a canteen on me and handed me some pills and I sat there sipping, until the multitude of aches resolved into a single dull throb.

"How you survived, Herr Oberleutnant, I have no idea, the turret is in ruins. Dieter and Otto were killed outright."

"Lucky, I suppose."

"Well, luckier than them at any rate," said Kurt nodding at the Matilda and I heard the hint of a rebuke in his voice. We had been comrades, friends, throughout the French campaign and rank meant little in that moment. In truth, I valued his candour.

"*Ja* Kurt. I know it was unwise to chase that Matilda, but you saw the command pennons? If we had captured… ach, but I should have disengaged. If I had, perhaps Dieter and Otto would still be alive…"

"And if my aunt had balls she'd be my uncle. At least you are man enough to recognise it, Siegfried. Many would not and war is an uncompromising teacher, it punishes even the smallest mistake. But what now?"

I drank more water as the pills began to take effect and my focus slowly returned. My body ached, but my command instincts were reasserting themselves and I managed to lever myself up and reach a sitting position. Kurt had lain me out in the cool of the sands, close to the remains of *Ingrid* but my vision still swam a little. I surveyed the panzer's broken shell without optimism.

The turret was shorn off and while the main body was intact, it was not going anywhere soon. It was indeed fortunate that it had not caught fire and burned us all, the tankers' perpetual terror, yet it was a wonder that any of us had made it out alive. But what now? What indeed? We were many kilometres from the main engagement and it was unlikely that anyone would come looking for us. They would presume we had been lost in the battle. I looked at Kurt, but he remained stoic, his eyes neutral, awaiting my command.

A small shape glided over in the semi-darkness and Little Hans, the kitten, bumped his head against my chin, winding his tail around my arm. He at least seemed to be suffering no ill effects and was evidently pleased to see me.

"Let's salvage what we can. Then, while the cool of the night lasts, we march."

CHAPTER TWO: SHADOWS IN THE MAELSTROM

We had recovered weapons, rations and water from the hulk of *Ingrid* and saying our goodbyes to our beloved Mark IV, we shouldered them as best we could. Jürgen greeted me with his habitual lop-sided grin and seemed largely unaffected by the experience, except for a slight limp. The young recover so quickly and when Death is your constant marching companion, you must learn to ignore the sound of his footsteps treading alongside your own. I suppose I could have ordered either of them to reconnoitre the Matilda, but I felt duty bound to see it for myself. I covered my nose with a scarf to suppress the odour of roasted flesh, but when I peered inside there was nothing useful there, just twisted metal and blackened corpses. Poor bastards.

So, I tucked Little Hans into my backpack where he peeped out over my shoulder and our trek through the night began. You might expect the desert to retain some residual heat from the day, but once the sun departs, it is a cold, desolate place, like the void of the heavens and we stamped and shivered to keep ourselves warm. Fortunately I had a compass in my pack and setting our course north by north west, we began the long plod back to our lines. Progress was slow, the sand filling your boots makes for unsure footing and weighs you down, sucking and dragging at your feet. Overhead, the stars stared down with supreme indifference and tramping through that waste, I was constantly reminded of our pitiful insignificance in the grander schemes of the universe.

We had walked for perhaps an hour or two, when the wind began to quicken. At first it was gentle, a careless zephyr which caressed the forehead, but soon it began to increase in volume, biting into the body, further hindering our progress. Then it grew in intensity again, carrying with it fine grains of sand, which clawed and rasped at the skin. We had to stop and wrap cloth around our faces lest the flesh be rubbed away and I ordered that we rope ourselves together, so that none became lost.

Fortunately my goggles afforded some protection and I took the lead as the sandstorm grew worse, the needle of the compass our only guide, visibility falling to a metre or two ahead. How long we journeyed like that I have no idea, for time became a meaningless concept as we struggled through that howling, abrasive void. The wind moaned like the call of the Valkyrie and any scrap of exposed flesh was scourged mercilessly. Little Hans had long since retreated deeper into the shelter of the pack.

We trudged on, even the stars blotted out now and our feet had been so accustomed to moving in the same direction, that for a while I hadn't consulted the compass and didn't notice when it started to behave in a most peculiar fashion. Yet when I looked now, the needle span and rotated, careering wildly on its axis, so that gauging an accurate reading was near impossible. I raised a fist to call a halt and we squatted down and I showed it to Kurt and Jürgen who greeted this strange phenomena with shrugs.

What could cause such a thing? There was little ready explanation but perhaps I should have felt more uneasiness then. I am a practical man and viewed it as a practical problem which required solving. Whatever the cause, the compass was next to useless in its current condition, so should we hunker down, stay put and wait for the storm to blow over or continue through the gale? Our tracks had been obliterated by the wind so there was no indication there, but I prided myself on my innate sense of direction and trusted my instincts to see us through. I made a chopping motion with my hand indicating we should go forward and our trek resumed.

It was not long before my decisiveness appeared to be rewarded, for within five minutes the winds began to slacken, the sandstorm part and the faintest traces of the night sky begin to peep through. Perhaps the tumult was beginning to blow itself out? Beneath my face mask I allowed myself a small smile. Five years in the military had taught me action is always preferable to inaction and even a swift wrong decision may prove better than a slower, more considered, correct one.

Then I saw them, dim shapes, vast shadows looming out of the relenting maelstrom ahead and I urged my companions onward. They were big enough to be structures certainly, so perhaps we could find shelter there? The compass was, if anything, more erratic now, the needle spinning wildly but we pressed on and then suddenly, we broke through the encircling squall, into an area of total calm. The winds dropped away and all was still, as if we were at the very eye of the storm.

It was a most unusual phenomenon. Not three metres from where we stood, the winds continued to blow with venom, yet in this 'eye', this circular column of tranquillity, all was placid. It was most unsettling. I looked up, following the lines of this funnel into the clear night sky above and while the blue-black firmament was comforting, it took me several moments to realise something was amiss. These were not any stars that I recognised. Strange alien suns leered back at me from the void, unusual galaxies and unfamiliar constellations. Being something of an amateur stargazer, as most poets are, I was well used to the familiar spread of the night sky, but this? This was a map of the heavens I did not recognise.

My head swam, yet there was no time to dwell upon it for what lay ahead already commanded my attention. There, apparently uncovered by the recent storm and still half wrapped in their sandy shrouds, were a series of vast stone-wrought structures nestling amongst the dunes. The uninformed eye might easily have mistaken them for pyramids I suppose, those long lost tombs of the pharaohs which litter the desert wastes. But I knew better, for these were not of Egyptian design, but rather more like the ancient ziggurats of the Incas or Aztecs of South

America—great stepped cairns adored with intricate, otherworldly carvings.

Astonishing as it was to discover these weird tombs several thousands of miles from where they should be, the presence of several vehicles parked in front of them was distinctly welcome. For I quickly recognised the distinctive outlines of an Sd.Kfz 250 half-track and several *Heer* troop trucks all decked out with fresh *Afrika Korps* livery. Off to one side, a large striped tent had been pitched in the shadow of the tombs and undoing my mask and removing my goggles, I turned to Kurt and Jürgen and indicated the parked convoy.

"It seems we won't have to walk all the way home, *Freunde.*" I said and their answering grins and slaps on each other's backs told their own story. Even Little Hans re-emerged from his refuge, but he gave a long querulous meow.

I cannot begin to describe to you the relief I felt, for honestly, before the break in the storm, I was beginning to wonder if I had miscalculated and the desert would become the final resting place for our bleached bones. In that moment, I forgot all my misgivings, forgot the odd behaviour of the compass and the strange vault overhead and was just happy to enjoy the salvation which had come unbidden to us. If only I had known then what was to come, I would have reversed course and headed straight back into the maelstrom without a backward glance.

Still, military protocol is always quick to re-assert itself and despite the presence of apparently friendly vehicles, I unshouldered my MP40 and moved cautiously toward them. There were no sentries on duty or signs of movement amongst the convoy, which was curious, for I would have expected any competent officer to have set a watch, especially in the midst of such a strange phenomena.

"Hallo!?" I shouted. "*Kameraden,* who is in command here?" But my only answer was the snarl of the surrounding wind. As we approached the half track, I noticed that it bore an additional insignia, a command badge bearing a curious device, a black circle with radial lightning flashes. It was familiar, where had I seen that before?

The question quickly became immaterial, for as we rounded the rear of the half-track and came upon the entrance to the ziggurat, things took on a far more disturbing turn. The entrance itself was remarkable enough, being a vast vaulted arch, carved with reliefs and intricately rendered sigils. I am not overly familiar with hieroglyphs but even to my untutored eye, these alien characters looked nothing like the ancient language of the Egyptians, but seemed to be comprised of lines and curves writhing in some unholy union

Yet disquieting as they were, this was not the sight which caused me to stifle a curse and quickly draw back. For there, lying on either side of the entrance were two sentries in desert fatigues, sprawled face down, their weapons fallen at their sides. "Kurt, Jürgen! Cover! Now!" I barked and both obeyed, moving into position by the half track to cover me while I scuttled over to examine the bodies.

The portal was dark and cavernous and for a moment I thought I saw a darker shadow detach itself and stir within, but it may just have been a trick of the light or indeed of the mind. I peered into the gaping depths again but saw nothing. Cautiously, with the toe of a boot, I turned one of the bodies over and it was all I could do to keep myself from crying aloud. Two years of this bloody war have inured me to all but the most grisly sights of the battlefield. One does not get used to them exactly, but one is able to endure them without flinching or remark. Yet this poor fellow, scarcely more than a boy, had died a death of uncommon agony.

His eyes gaped wide, swollen with pain or terror and they stared sightless straight up into the heavens. His skin was mottled and flecked with a strange purple-yellow hue as if it were bruised and haemorrhaging from within. His features had been distorted beyond the normal limits and there was an unpleasant acrid odour rising from his body which caused me to recoil.

There was a sound like a demon spitting and a sharp pain in my shoulder and I almost jumped a metre in the air! But it was only Little Hans, his back arched and his hair standing on end, spitting fury, before he buried himself into the backpack again. I let out a great sigh and breathed deeply to calm my racing pulse.

The corpse bore no bullet holes or other marks of battle, so what in the name of heaven could inflict such wounds on a man? I checked the other body and found it in a similar condition, swollen and empurpled. I signalled Kurt to come over and take a look.

"*Scheisse! Mein Gott*, that is not a pretty sight."

"*Ja*, but what could cause such terrible wounds?"

"Well if you'll listen to my advice, Herr Oberleutnant, it's no business of ours. These trucks? The same insignia as that strange SS detachment on the voyage over. I didn't like the look of them then and I don't like the look of them now. Whatever they are up to here, I say they are welcome to it. Perhaps we should just commandeer one of these lorries and leave?"

"Usually I would quote duty and common cause with fellow troops of the Fatherland, but something about this place inclines me to believe you're right, Kurt. This is one mystery that can solve itself. Go, see if you can find something to cover them and let's get out of here before we meet a similar fate."

"That is one order I have no problem with obeying, Herr Oberleutnant," said Kurt as he went to search the trucks.

Perhaps you think this a cowardly response? A dereliction of duty, gentlemen? Perhaps it was, but all I can say is you were not there. You did not see the awful, ghastly, condition of those men, those bloated corpses transformed by something which seemed to have no readily explicable origin. Combine that with the bizarre phenomena we had encountered and believe me, I had little hesitation in wanting to get away from that place.

I mentioned that I have seen many horrors under fire? Well yes, I have, many times and I have no need to regale you with tales of my courage. One does not need to have seen *Nosferatu*, *Fear* or *The Cabinet of Dr Caligari* or a thousand other tales of horror to be able to read those runes: a compass gone wild, strange stars above, a complex of ancient temples many thousands of miles from where they should be?

If you had placed all these ingredients in a horror film, the audience would have howled at the heroes to turn and flee and I was of a similar mind. I wanted no part of it. My duty as I saw it was to get my men home and return to fight another day.

Yet our hand was forced, by fate perhaps and in the end we had little choice but to stay.

Kurt returned shaking his head.

"There are no keys, either in the half track or the trucks."

"Damn." I bent down and holding my nose, quickly searched the sentries' pockets. "Nothing on these two either and we're not going to get very far on foot with the compass playing the devil."

"Observe," said Kurt, pointing to the ground in front of the portal. There are many tracks there, all leading into the darkness. None come back the other way.

"That means there is only one place the keys can be."

"In there?"

"In there."

"*Verdammte Scheisse!*" this time it was my turn to curse.

We found electric torches in the trucks and once we had covered the unfortunate sentries with a tarpaulin, I took the lead as we walked into that primeval tomb. The torch beams were powerful, but seemed to cut only so far into the gloom before being swallowed up by the immense darkness of that ancient place. I found my finger had slipped unbidden onto the trigger of my machine pistol as we proceeded down a vast corridor which spanned many metres across and sloped gently into the interior of the ziggurat. It was constructed of huge blocks of dressed limestone which were fitted together with a precision which seemed almost inhuman, and perhaps it was just the oppressive atmosphere of that place, but I seemed to feel rather than see, things wriggling and slithering beyond our feeble lights. It was then I suppose I first began to consider seriously whether this place had been constructed by the pharaohs or something older and far darker.

On we walked and for some reason, comfort perhaps, I still occasionally turned my head to view the portal behind us, which slowly diminished until it was just a distant, pale rectangle which could scarcely be distinguished from the surrounding shadows. It seemed to grow warmer too as we penetrated deeper into that place and an unusual smell began to pervade the air, an odour I couldn't identify, but didn't much care for; though if pressed, I would say it had an almost reptilian quality. We pushed on silently, the insignificant tap tap of our footsteps the only sound in those hollow walls, like thieves intruding upon eternity. I didn't dare break the sepulchral silence of the place by calling out, but the immense stillness was beginning to play on my nerves.

"Herr Oberleutnant?" Kurt whispered and I was relieved to hear another human voice.

"*Ja?*"

"I do not like the feel of this place, no not at all."

"Nor I Kurt."

"Perhaps we should consider turning back?"

"We need those keys, if there were any other way…" I let my words hang there in the silence

"Forgive me sir," interjected Jürgen. "But is that light, there, ahead?" I strained and squinted and was forced to agree. His youthful eyes had indeed detected a faint flicker in the gloom.

"It seems the decision is made for us. Kurt, take point and keep your weapon ready. Who knows what we will discover there?"

We extinguished our torches and followed Kurt as he stalked forward in the darkness, moving quietly over the stone flagged floor. As we drew closer, the light became brighter, outlining another vast portal marked with that same writhing script which afforded glimpses into the chamber beyond. Kurt needed no orders from me to direct him and snuck forward like the wily old infantry scout he had once been, hugging the wall so that he remained hidden in shadow until he gained the corner where doorway met corridor. Quickly, he stole a glance into the chamber, then ducked back again and I could hear my heart racing in my ears as I awaited a cry of discovery. None came, the silence remained unbroken and he tilted his head around for a longer, more thorough look. My finger tightened on the outside of the trigger guard, but there was no reaction and after turning on his light again and sweeping the chamber thoroughly, Kurt stood up and beckoned us forward.

"*Mein Gott,* Herr Oberleutnant, you had better come and see this."

The central chamber was huge, a vast space carved from weighty limestone blocks far richer than those that had marked the entranceway. Here, they were truly titanic in stature and no longer simple dressed stone, but carved with the same serpentine glyphs and sigils which decorated the portal entrance. A low level luminescence seeped from strange marker stones embedded at irregular intervals in the walls, allowing us to see a little despite the natural murkiness of the place.

In the centre of this expanse, a dais dominated, rising a couple of metres above ground level and set with a series of what looked like marble thrones, though some appeared not naturally suited to a normal human posture. Behind these thrones, a vast frieze of strange half-man, half-snake-like beings writhed in eerie relief and on pedestals on either side, esoteric statues and figures brooded and intermingled in ways that were not entirely wholesome to behold. Completing the scene was a huge brass gong, complete with a device for striking it, which looked like a coiled serpent.

It was a most unusual and disquieting scene in itself, for this was no ordinary tomb of the pharaohs or I was a Dutchman – and being from Bavaria, I most certainly was no Lowlander. Yet bizarre as it was, this tableau was not what had caused Kurt's disquiet, for there, spread around the base of the dais, their bodies twisted and contorted in the same attitudes as the sentries we had found outside, were some twenty German soldiers. We had found the SS, or at least, what remained of them.

I listened intently, but not a sound interrupted the stygian blackness and as my eyes slowly adjusted to the low level light within, I could see nothing stir in the galleries and gantries which surrounded the central dais. The bodies were lying right in the middle of the chamber, in a horribly exposed position, but we needed those keys and we would not gain them by remaining where we were. I signalled Kurt and Jürgen to cover me from the entranceway and with the softest of steps, I crept across to where the bodies lay, my ears pricked for the slightest sound.

I moved from man to man, or corpse to corpse as it turned out, for they all bore the same distorted features, twisted limbs and mottled discolorations of the skin as their comrades outside, suggesting they had suffered the same horrible agonies. I rifled through the pockets of the nearest, fearful of touching them in case I picked up any contagion.

Damn, nothing and sweating profusely, my hands fumbled, feeling clumsy and uncoordinated. I must move with haste lest whatever had ambushed these poor unfortunates returned to inflict the same fate on me. I came to the next group and as I patted the shorts pocket of a rather fat sergeant, there, at last! I heard a tell-tale jingle and felt inside, removing a set of keys. Truck or half-track it didn't matter, as long as it would hasten our retreat away from this cursed place, I did not care one iota. Grinning, I held the keys up to show Kurt and Jürgen, and their answering smiles told of their own relief.

I was just on the point of creeping back when a deep, lingering groan came from one of the bodies nearby. I almost leapt out of my skin, but instinct took over and I hit the floor, bringing up the machine pistol, pointing at the source of the sound. For a moment, all was still, then the groan came again and it sounded like a man with the schnapps hangover from hell. I raised an eye over the end of the sight.

"Hello, would you be so good as to lend me a hand?" The voice was weak and I did not recognise the words but the language was most definitely British.

"Identify yourself!" I shouted and even to my own ears my voice sounded stretched, hollow.

"Würden Sie bitte so freundlich sein und mir helfen?"

This time the words were in flawless German and cautiously, I raised myself up and stalked over to examine their source. There, at the bottom of the pile and half buried beneath the SS bodies slumped inertly on top of him, was the head and shoulders of a most curious looking individual.

He wore a black beret with what looked like a paratrooper's badge, though from no regiment I recognised and he had on an aviator's leather jacket, as I had seen our own bomber crews wear, though it was devoid of any rank badge or markings. A rather equine face was framed by long, curiously pale, and very un-military hair which fanned out on the ground underneath him. His eyes were shut tight, the face contorted in a grimace of deep pain and just like the SS, his skin was flecked and discoloured black and purple. Yet on his face the markings seemed to ripple and flow across the surface, as if some infernal internal struggle were going on.

I dropped my weapon and placed my pack on the ground, loosening the gag which constrained his mouth. Then I made to move the bodies pinning him there, but his lips opened a little and teeth gritted, he said.

"No, water …please." The words were strangely forceful, compelling almost, and I moved the gag aside, held the canteen to his mouth and he drank it greedily, gorging on the liquid. In a moment, the canteen was half empty and then he began to cough and retch, so that I feared he was choking and that ironically, I had half drowned him.

I began to roll away the corpses which pinned him and forgetting the need for quiet, called on Kurt and Jürgen to lend a hand. In seconds they were at my side, helping me shift the dead weight surrounding him and all the time this man hacked and sputtered as if he were expelling every last gasp of oxygen from his lungs.

We heaved the last corpse away and as he lay there, I watched as blue-black, necrotic hues danced across his features a final time, before seeping out through his pores as shadowy wisps which burned away before our eyes. The man lay very still, very quiet and for a moment I thought we had been too late and those pale features now relaxed in a death-like repose. But then his eyes flicked open and with just a trace of amusement, he said.

"*Danke,* just what the doctor ordered, though I would advise you not to sample any of the medicine I have had recently forced upon me."

I looked at Kurt and Jürgen who seemed equally astonished by this strange fellow, but in a trice he had picked himself up, the bonds which had held him fell away like gossamer and he was dusting himself down, apparently free of the convulsions which had gripped him just moments before. He stooped for a moment and retrieved a set of charms and amulets from one of the SS corpses which looked vaguely Egyptian in origin and immediately hung them around his neck.

"Who are you? How did you get here? What happened to these soldiers? " I demanded.

"My, you are full of questions aren't you? Understandable I suppose, so let's take them in order: how I got here was as a *guest* of the Black Sun you see laying before you. What happened to them? Well, that will require a slightly more detailed explanation and you may not believe it, even when I tell you. As for my name? Well, you can call me Seraph, let's say Captain Seraph, yes, I suppose that would do, lately of the British Eighth army, or as you most likely know us, *Die Wüstenratten,* the Desert Rats."

"Very well, Captain Seraph," I said, raising my weapon. "You may now consider yourself my prisoner and I demand that you..."

"A prisoner of the panzers, hm? Well, I've had worse and recently too. Your comrades – or perhaps that's the wrong word – well, they weren't exactly the most hospitable of captors." He looked down at the bodies surrounding us with a faint disdain before continuing.

"However, I would like to point out as a matter of fact that you're every bit as much a prisoner here as I am." He nodded indicating behind me and to my astonishment, where there had once been an open space leading back down the corridor to the open desert, now there stood a wall of solid stone.

"I'd also add," said Captain Seraph raising an eyebrow laden with meaning. "It's neither polite nor especially clever to wave a weapon at the one man who might, just might, be your best chance of getting out of here alive."

I cursed, not able to decide whether to be infuriated by his glib remarks or impressed by his apparent *sang froid*.

"Clearly you have many questions," said Captain Seraph. "Allow me to fill in some of the blanks."

CHAPTER THREE: FILLING IN THE BLANKS

"Please don't be so naive as to expect me to disclose my sources or how I came to know any of this, just believe me when I say my information is impeccable. A short while ago, Section E, the department which I work for, received intelligence that a small detachment of this Black Sun brigade were heading to North Africa.

"This piqued my interest, for the Black Sun attract me like honey attracts flies. You may have travelled with some of them on your journey across the Med I dare say, but it's unlikely you'll have heard of this particular unit before, no?

"Let me fill you in then with some of the background. There's a certain cabal of high ranking German officers who exert a great deal of influence on your beloved *Führer*. They have persuaded him that certain arcane resources may become extremely useful to him during the course of this conflict. The Black Sun are the unit charged with seeking out and securing these artefacts for the greater glory of your Fatherland. I see the scepticism writ large on your faces: tank men rightly place their trust in armour-piercing shells and steel, but look at where you now stand and the bodies of these troops and tell me if you think this has anything to do with conventional warfare?

"A day or so ago, I was deep behind your lines, observing this very unit as they left El Agheila sheltering beneath the wings of your Rommel's lightning strike. Impressive fellow that, I fear he may cause us no end of trouble before the business is concluded here.

"Be that as it may, I took no part in the main offensive, for the more shadowy areas of the war are where I operate best and with Abdullah, an old Arab friend and some of his allies acting as guides, I trailed this group into the great wastes by camel."

"By camel?" Kurt looked sceptical.

"You'd be wise not to underestimate the camel, Feldwebel, a most hardy beast and eminently more suited to conducting desert warfare than armour. Nevertheless, we followed at what I thought was a discreet distance, though evidently perhaps not discreet enough, until the Black Sun pitched camp outside. As the light began to fade, there seemed to be some sort of intensive preparations going on inside the commander's tent and I must say my natural curiosity got the better of me. I'm an inquisitive fellow at the best of times and I was dying to discover what could have drawn the Black and particularly their fetching commander, Fräulein Liesel Böhm, to this remote locale. I did not have to wait long to find out."

"A woman? In charge of an SS unit? Unheard of! You are a poor liar, Englishman," said Kurt.

"I assure you, I am no liar, Feldwebel and 'Sweet Liesel' is no mere Fräulein, but a quite lethal and ruthless Nazi operative who carries the field rank of Obersturmführer. A most remarkable not to say deadly young woman, who is quite capable of sacrificing every man under her command to attain her ends." He raised an eyebrow, indicating the bodies around us.

"And what ends are those, Captain?" I asked a little more politely than Kurt.

"Allow me to come to that in my own good time my dear fellow, for this tale bears some retelling. Anyway, as I watched from a dune nearby with my Arab friends, something was evidently afoot, for as the final embers of the sun ebbed from the sky, the very desert itself began to stir.

The sand shifted and eddied, strong winds sprang from the ether and a most unnatural storm was suddenly brewing. I would bet a farthing to a guinea that Fräulein Böhm was behind it, for even though she believes herself gifted in the darker arts, her party also consisted of several shall we say *forcibly conscripted* fellows, Ukrainian scholars, occultists and the like, who would serve her in conjuring the ritual … and what lay beyond it.

The storm grew in intensity tearing at our faces and skin – no doubt you were forced to endure its privations as you made your way here – and Abdullah's friends began chuntering and clutching their totems protectively, muttering charms against the dark. My Arab friend was in a right fug, for he is not used to such spectacles and is understandably wary of the power of such dark sorcery. Nevertheless, it was critical I take a closer look, so advising them to report back to base, I used the cover of the winds to work my way closer and inveigled myself inside the perimeter. Handily, I have a talent for remaining inconspicuous, at least to conventional eyes and I was soon able to eavesdrop on what Sweet Liesel was plotting.

I had judged my moment well for they were just approaching the climax of the ritual. Beneath the canvas, they had gathered around what looked like an altar of strange, unholy design, all unearthly angles, slithering sigils and forked intersections, a little like the dais you see before you here. I recognised it immediately as an artefact sometimes known as the Fangs of Set, though it also has many other names.

Gathered around it, a group of hooded, cowled men were intoning a monstrous dirge in a language I had not heard in a long time. Nor has this Earth, for its low, sibilant phrasing carried whispers of an existence millennia departed and I had not thought to hear it again from the mouths of living men. There, overseeing them with a curved blade clutched in her hand was Liesel Böhm, her eyes fierce with dark witch light and tinged with a kind of lust that is not wholesome to behold.

As the chanting reached its zenith, the naked, spread-eagled captive lashed to the altar began to moan in terror and I knew what must come next. Liesel leaned over his terrified face, almost tenderly at first, planting a kiss on each eye, then finally, a long lingering one on his lips. Raising the blade far above her head, she plunged the dagger down into his heart's blood so that it ran as red as her flaming hair, spilling over the mouths and tongues of the altar and running in rivulets along the spokes of the great arcane symbol which had been daubed below it. His cry pierced the night, descending into bubbling gasps as his life drained away and then there was an instant of almost perfect stillness as even the winds themselves became quiescent.

It was almost imperceptible at first, a slight tremor but quickly it grew deeper, stronger, building in intensity. Close by, the very sands began to tremble, shift and change. With a noise like the Earth grinding its teeth, great stones broke through the surface, pushing their way up through the sand like fingers. Walls and ramparts followed as if some ancient titan were shaking off its shroud until finally they rose before us, three ziggurats of ancient Lemuria which had not seen the sun's rays for nigh on seven millennia.

How she had pinpointed their location I had no idea, but Sweet Liesel is a resourceful woman and there are many dark places in the world which know her intimate touch. The evidence was there before my very eyes but still I was astounded, so staggered in fact with calculating the implications that I must have let my guard down for a moment. The next thing I knew, the muzzle of a machine pistol was planted firmly against my temple and one of those delightful Black Sun chaps was inviting me to *hände hoch* and to be mighty *schnell!* about it.

I was marched unceremoniously into the presence of the delectable Obersturmführer herself and I could tell she was not best pleased to see me. I would have attempted to dissemble, but my appearance is somewhat distinctive and unfortunately known amongst the ranks of the Black Sun, for does not the snake know of the mongoose, even if it has never encountered one? Sometime, I must think about addressing that particular weakness, but Sweet Liesel came straight to the point.

"Well what have we here? A drowned desert rat? No, I think this can only be the remarkable Herr Seraph who I have heard so much about from my mentor Ludwig von Obertorff. I am curious, what brings you to our little theatre of operations, Herr Seraph?"

"I might ask you the same question. What are you doing with that altar?"

"That is no concern of yours."

"Sorry, beg to differ, my dear. Opposing evil is always my concern, especially when it meddles with forces which are not only beyond its comprehension but also its control."

"Do not make the mistake of underestimating me, Herr Seraph, I know what I am doing. But perhaps you would be so kind as to tell me one good reason why I should not have you executed immediately?"

"You know, you'd think that kind of challenge would bring out the best in a fellow, but to be honest, if I were in your position, I can't think of a single one..."

"Fool, I am not in the habit of throwing away anything which may prove useful. Fortunately I am not so rash as to execute one of the Fatherland's most implacable, not to say knowledgeable enemies, when a use might still be found for him. Scharführer, search him, strip him of any trinkets or devices you find, for he is a most devious fellow. Once that's done, bind and gag him so that we are not troubled by that pretty, eloquent mouth of his. Don't trouble yourself about being gentle, but make sure you do no permanent damage. Once that's done, hobble him. Allow him to walk, but no more than a shuffle. I wouldn't want such a valuable asset to go astray."

So I was trussed and bound like a sacrificial lamb, thrown in the back of one of the trucks and kept under the watchful eye of Black Sun sentries, while Sweet Liesel and her cabal mopped up the aftermath of the ritual. Within a quarter of an hour, they were packed and ready to go, ready so they thought, to penetrate deep into the heart of this fell edifice."

"Ach," spat Jürgen. "He is either a liar, a madman, or both, Herr Oberleutnant. Why should we listen to this nonsense any more? These SS bodies have more than enough *Stielhandgranaten*, let me rig them together and we will blast our way out of this place." At this prospect, Captain Seraph looked horrified.

"I would not advise that, Herr Oberleutnant. Not only will that have little practical effect, but it will almost certainly cause the inhabitants of this place to come running, or rather slithering, down on us like the vengeance of Hades. Let me assure you... you, we, do not want that."

"Inhabitants?" I enquired.

"My tale is nearly concluded," said Captain Seraph. "Indulge me for a couple of minutes more, then all will become clear and then you can decide what to do next." Jürgen was clearly not enthralled by this prospect and I was undecided about this strange fellow and his wild tale. Yet here we stood in a place and situation for which I had no ready explanation. When I looked to him for guidance, Kurt shrugged.

"It can do no harm to hear him out, sir." I nodded and Captain Seraph resumed his tale.

"A short while later, I was unceremoniously ejected from the backboards, dragged to my feet and pushed, kicked and shoved to the main entrance of the ziggurat which now stood invitingly open. Sweet Liesel was there and bold, saucy girl that she is, had no qualms about plunging straight into the heart of this tomb. No doubt you have deduced that this is no mere resting place of the pharaohs, but something from a very different age. Maany aeons ago, not far from here, there was another city, one called Sethopolis in the human tongue, although its inhabitants call it by another almost unpronounceable name, which claimed a dark hegemony over what we now call the entire Arabian peninsula. As far as I can tell this is a caravanserai of that unhallowed place, an outpost which has slept beneath the sands for millennia. As far as mankind is concerned, it would have been better left there.

Yet Sweet Liesel must pursue her aims and damn the consequences. Soon we had left the howling storm behind us and plunged deep into the heart of this place, this tomb of the aeons, with her sorcerers bearing the Fangs of Set before them like a processional offering.

All was silent at first, quiet as the grave, but as we penetrated deeper the Black Sun had to persuade her pet sorcerers at bayonet point, for no doubt they suspected what foulness lurked inside. Reluctantly they obeyed, carrying that altar before them all the while. Trussed and gagged, I had little option but to follow and I could issue no admonition, no warning, to dissuade her from this rashest of courses. Finally, we stood assembled before the dais you see here and Sweet Liesel commanded me brought forward.

"So here we are then, Herr Seraph, anything you'd like to get off your chest before we proceed?" She laughed cruelly, full well knowing I could say nothing, gagged as I was. "What's the matter? Cat got your tongue?" She taunted.

It was at this point that Little Hans, perhaps summoned by the mention of a fellow feline, chose to make his presence known by clambering from out of my pack and perching on my shoulder. Captain Seraph suddenly twinkled, enquired "Who this little fellow was?"' and when informed, said. "Well that is fortuitous, for I am almost inordinately fond of cats." His affection was obviously reciprocated, for Little Hans leapt onto his shoulder and began purring loudly. Scratching the creature's ears contentedly, the captain continued.

"Sweet Liesel wasted no more time baiting me and the chief of her captive sorcerers was soon up on that dais and ready to strike that great gong which you see there. A nod from his mistress and the note rang out, echoing through this great hollow space with a deep atonal clang, chasing back on itself along the passageways, corridors and galleries which surround this chamber. For a merciful time, there was no response, but then the *other* sounds began, a slithering and slipping like parched scales rasping across stone, or the sibilant hiss of the sands.

Now they drew closer, like a great horde of shadows, a swarm of suggestive, serpentine sounds, so that even the Black Sun became unnerved and drew close to one another, cocking their weapons and forming a defensive posture—for what little good it would do them. The sorcerers drew back too, their chief scuttling from the platform as if scalded and he joined his fellows in quaking before this unseen menace. Sweet Liesel though, I will give her credit, was magnificent, like an ice maiden or a Valkyrie, supremely, sublimely unconcerned, arrogant and aloof, secure in the secret knowledge she thought would protect her. Alone she stood, bold and unafraid, while all around her quailed.

Then, when the din was at the very threshold and I thought they must flood into the chamber and overwhelm us, all at once the sounds ceased and silence reigned for a long moment.

I am gifted with extraordinary sight, but even I did not wholly see their coming. One moment the dais was empty, the next a group of tall, robed humanoids stood there, their arms folded in anger or judgement it was difficult to say. Their garments were marked with ancient, disquieting symbols and they were festooned with jewellery of an intricate and ingenious design. Yet where one might expect to see human heads and faces, instead there were the flickering countenances of *Schlangen*, snakes: python, cobra, adder, viper, each representing a subset of the order *serpentes*, a congregation of the deadliest nobles and sorcerers of their most uncanny species.

For these were serpent kind, scions of lost Valusia, representatives of that race which had once held dominion over the continents of man and had only been defeated by the most strenuous efforts of the sons of Atlantis.

For long aeons they had slept in their lair, retreating into the dark, moist corners of the earth to await a propitious time to rise again. Why Sweet Liesel had chosen to prod this particular nest, I had no definite idea but I was beginning to form a notion. For serpent kind are masters of all manner of deadly poisons and toxins and if she could harness just one small portion of their formidable arcane knowledge, then it might be readily adapted for your Führer's baser purposes..."

"Baser purposes?" spat Jürgen. "As if this tale weren't already fantastical enough! You want us to believe that these Black Sun led by this improbable woman came here to learn about poison from *Schlangenmenschen*? Pah, this proves you lie. Even if we accept this outrageous tale, the Wehrmacht does not use poisons or gas anymore. They are of no use on the modern battlefield, not in the age of Blitzkrieg," he added triumphantly.

"Oh, but it won't be the *Heer* my boy, not them, not them at all and it won't be for use on the battlefield either. Eichmann and Heydrich want it reserved for use in their own *domestic* horrors, you see. It promises to be a thousand times more potent than their current solution."

"Ach, now I know you are deranged, Captain Seraph, are you suggesting we would use it on our own population? Ridiculous..."

"You have been away on duty for how many years? I imagine you hear little of what is truly going on on the home front? Believe me or not, it is of no consequence, but understand this: one day every German will hold it a shame to the soul of their gallant nation that they attached their fortunes to that Nazi madman's ignoble star."

Jürgen glowered and seemed on the very point of raising his MP40 at the captain, but Kurt intervened and gently pushed the weapon down.

"A fantastic tale indeed, Captain Seraph." I said, "As you say, we are simple soldiers and not familiar with the intricacies of higher policy, or indeed this arcane world in which you say we suddenly find ourselves. But finish your tale and then we will decide what we decide."

The captain nodded and continued.

"While her entourage cowered from those silent, imposing figures, Sweet Liesel herself was unabashed and strode forth and addressed them directly in a manner which was at once both remarkable and impressive. Serpent kind's tongue is near impossible for human vocal chords to master, but, clever girl, she addressed them in the ancient speech of Atlantis, which they were bound to recognise. Now, I'm no slouch myself with languages myself but even I admit she had a facility that was remarkable."

"Serpent lords, I offer you greetings and salutations from my master, Adolf Hitler, lord of the modern world and *Führer* of the great German nation."

The serpents regarded her, unblinking.

"For long centuries you have slept, but I have awoken you now to propose a grand alliance, a mutually advantageous pact which would benefit both our peoples. The nations of the world already lie trembling before the armies of my master, but with your help he can accelerate and cement the triumph of his thousand year Reich. In return he offers you a bargain, the resurrection of your ancient kingdom of Valusia and dominion over the African continent, which you may rule as you see fit."

At this bold speech the serpent lords looked to each other and although no words were spoken, it was evident they were communicating amongst themselves. This continued for a short while and then the cobra-headed creature spoke in a voice like a jagged whisper.

"And what would thisss Hitler, thisss Führer ask of us in return?"

"Knowledge, a small portion of your accumulated wisdom is all he desires to speed along a certain problem that requires an ... accelerated solution. That would constitute a first act of faith, to prove we could work together.

"After that? Well now he is almost master of Europe, but his gaze must soon venture eastwards and once the great Soviet steppes are conquered, the New World awaits. Understand, this is inevitable but your knowledge combined with our advanced technology and military prowess would speed the process considerably."

"And what if we refussse to share this knowledge?"

"The alternative? Well let us say I found your lair without undue difficulty and there are many more adept than I in the *Schwarze Sonne*. You note I make no threat, for your wisdom is legendary and your knowledge that of the ages. Yet without your cooperation, I would say your future may not be a felicitous one."

At this, the creatures looked from one to the other again and it was easy for those who can see to discern the intense telepathic traffic passing between those inscrutable reptilian faces. At length this seemed to subside and the serpent lord who wore the aspect of a python stepped forward. Its tongue flickered, sampling the air and its third parietal eye seemed to come alive, blazing with fury.

"Foolish human wretch, you think to intimidate us with your scarcely veiled threats? Your lies are as transsssparent to us as your feeble mind. You would take our knowledge, oh yesss, use our insssights but there would be no place for our people in a world ruled by *your* master.

"Do you think we sssleep so blindly in the dark? That we are unaware of the wider course of eventsss? We see the way the world burnsss because of your master's ambition and we wish no part of it, for the fate of the ssserpent is not governed by man's conception of time.

"You tell us that you are no adept and that isss true, but others will come to disturb us? We think not, Liesssel Böhm, for we see from your own pathetically weak mind that your ambition prevented you from sharing your knowledge with your comrades of this Black Sun.

"Yet we thank you for bringing us the gift of the Fangsss of Set, an artefact which woke us from our slumber and which will enable us to sssubtly extend our influence in the present, while remaining hidden from the world of mortal men. If you had any conception of its true nature you would have left it buried in the vault where you found it and run sssscreaming, rather than bringing it to us here.

"Your mensss' lives are forfeit, but you will ssserve us down the long aeons until we are ready to re-emerge and claim our birthright. Though we are curious to discover what an eternity of sssuffering and sssservitude will do to your frail consciousness."

At this the snake lord gave a long protracted hiss and all hell broke loose, for while he had been berating Sweet Liesel, his minions had subtly manoeuvred themselves into position to spring their trap. Now they struck in a welter of fang and fury, spitting venom and biting at the Black Sun troopers, who, taken by surprise and panicking, loosed off their own weapons.

For a moment all was chaos as Black Sun trooper grappled with serpent kind in a bitter close-quarters combat. But the serpents were too many and too quick and the Black Sun were quickly overrun, going down writhing in their death agonies as the poison took hold, succumbing to the fury of the snake.

Still bound, I could do little to protect myself and was bitten many times. As I toppled, the venom coursing its potent way through my veins, the last thing I saw was Sweet Liesel and her pet sorcerers being led away by the snake lords. The rest? Well that I think you know better than I, for I remember nothing more until you discovered me."

"How then are you alive, when the Black Sun are not?" asked Kurt.

"Fortunately, I am naturally a little more resistant to toxins than your average fellow," shrugged Captain Seraph. "It's something peculiar to my blood and ancestry, but even so, the snake's poison is potent and quite overwhelmed me for a time."

Now that the captain's tale was complete I nodded, passed him my canteen again and drew Kurt and Jürgen a little distance away to talk in private. The British officer amused himself by playing with Little Hans, who seemed delighted by his attentions.

"He is clearly deranged sir. Sorcery, serpent lords, magical artefacts from the past? These are not the workings of a rational mind," said Jürgen.

"Yet something killed these Black Sun troopers, something extraordinary, those horrified expressions, those strange markings. You saw those strange vapours creeping from his skin. "

"Gas? Some kind of nerve agent?"

"Perhaps, but the British don't use that kind of material any more than we do."

"So what exactly is capable of destroying an entire SS unit like that?"

"I've no idea, but I'm in no great hurry to find out."

"And what of this place? It gives me the shivers, I wish we had taken our chances in the desert."

"I too, yet here we find ourselves with no immediate way out apart from attempting to blast a hole through what looks like solid rock. Just how did that tunnel manage to seal itself anyway? It's uncanny. There's more here than meets the eye."

"Undoubtedly, but he says he knows a way out, or at least he thinks he does."

"Can we trust him?"

"Trust him? Maybe not but we can trust his self interest. As long as he can find a way out of here for us all, that will suffice."

They both looked to me for a decision.

"Very well, if the captain can find us another way out of here, let's take it. After that we can decide what to do. If he fails or attempts to betray us, we can always make our way back here and give the grenades a try. At least we have the keys now, so we won't be walking home. " I addressed myself to the curious British officer.

"Captain Seraph. We are decided, we have no wish to disturb this tomb's... inhabitants. If you know of another route out of here, perhaps you would be good enough to show us the way?"

"Capital old boy. That I will. Let's get going. "

"How will you know where to lead us, Captain, if you have never been here before?" asked Jürgen sullenly.

"Oh that's easy," said Captain Seraph. "We'll just follow the bodies."

CHAPTER FOUR: THE SONG OF THE SNAKE

So after a short pause, during which we took his advice and rearmed ourselves with some of the Black Sun's more exotic looking weaponry and all the explosives we could carry, Captain Seraph took the lead and we began our journey into the depths. If I had known all that was to transpire thereafter, I would probably have risked bringing the roof down and much more besides.

Behind the dais was another great archway and we were soon through it and plunging down into another shallow tunnel leading further into the heart of the place. We had walked perhaps fifty paces when Captain Seraph suddenly held up his fist, as if sensing something at the junction up ahead and we stopped in our tracks while he stalked forward. He glided his way up to the intersection and then apparently satisfied, straightened up and regarding the unseen corridor intently, waved us forward.

"Poor fellow. The snake lords' handiwork undoubtedly," said the captain dispassionately. Even to a soldier's hardened eye this was a macabre sight. The man had been bound and gagged, stripped naked and suspended upside down. The veins on his arms had been opened precisely and his throat cut, so that all his life blood drained out into a great bronze vessel below, where it bubbled ominously.

"A sign of the beings we are dealing with," said Captain Seraph, "and if any of you doubted it before, this is the kind of mercy we can expect from them."

The captain padded on without giving the victim another glance, but none of us were able to pass that ghastly sight with such equanimity. Whatever the truth of Captain Seraph's fantastical tale, someone or perhaps something had inflicted this unnatural torment on that poor man and I think it was then that I first began to believe our enemy might not be wholly natural in origin.

Down we went and slowly came into a complex set of interweaving tunnels and junctions that intersected at random. Captain Seraph quickly came to resemble nothing so much as a hunting hound, one of our own Weimaraners, those lanky faithful grey ghosts, for often he would pause and scent the air before deciding on which direction to take. Once in a while our journey would be punctuated by another one of those macabre markers, an unfortunate sorcerer who had been slaughtered and hung like a *schwein* in a butcher's shop, the steady drip drip of his life blood a staccato timepiece. The captain passed these markers without pause or comment, but I could not suppress a shudder and I felt Kurt and Jürgen tense and stiffen at each successive bloody 'milestone'.

Soon, we were deep into the labyrinth and had taken so many twists, turns and double backs that it was difficult to gauge where we were going, or indeed how far we had come.

Our torches flickered across unadorned stone corridors and featureless walls, past ghostly untenanted chambers, some still half filled with sand or the detritus of the ages. Sometimes fearsome statues and complex otherworldly geometry adorned these rooms but at others, there was simply plain, undressed stone, as featureless as glass. We passed huge brazen mirrors with dark surfaces that distorted and contorted our reflections, and trudged past giant idols of serpents intertwined with serpent men eerily reflecting Captain Seraph's story and only added to our disquiet. In one otherwise desolate room, there was a huge multi-layered frieze depicting a battle between the serpent people and primitive men, with the humans being urged on by what looked like a giant cat and the snake men led by an enormous snake god.

Occasionally smaller tunnels that were barely knee height or lower branched off, so that one would have to crawl on one's belly to use them and I started to wonder if perhaps there might actually be some truth to Captain Seraph's outlandish tale. There seemed no rhyme or reason to this place and the overwhelming impression was of a giant alien burrow, still and daunting in its otherworldliness.

Onward we crept, going deeper and darker into that dread place and the stillness started to become oppressive, like a weight that hung heavy upon the soul. We moved slowly but inexorably downward, inward toward the very heart of the tomb. Old soldiers have an instinct for these things or else they do not become old soldiers.

The silence began to take on an even more ominous quality now and occasionally my instincts would bristle, as if they sensed something watching us from the shadows, hiding just out of sight. Yet every time I directed my torch, there was nothing there. Kurt felt it too, I know, for once in a while I would catch his expression in a reflected beam and it was full of a kind of creeping, nameless dread that I had not seen even in our most desperate moments under fire. Only Jürgen seemed unaffected and he plunged onward after the captain with the blithe optimism of youth.

Now we came to a great junction, a space with myriad corridors and galleries leading off in all directions. Captain Seraph stopped, seemingly perplexed for the moment and I knew I must seize my chance.

"Captain."

"Hm?" He appeared to have heard me, although his attention constantly wandered.

"Captain Seraph!" I hissed. "Where are you taking us?"

"Why, just as promised, I'm leading us out of here."

"Yet your road leads us away from the surface, not toward it."

"Why yes." He sounded surprised.

"What?!" spat Jürgen. "You are deliberately leading us further into this place? Let me shoot him now, sir, I can find the way back, if you let me try the grenades..."

The captain looked hurt by this accusation.

"Let me assure you I *am* taking us out of here, by the only way there is. In order to tread that path, we have to proceed further into the pyramid, retrieve the altar and rescue Sweet Liesel, if she still lives."

"What?!" This time it was Kurt who erupted, his nerves finally fraying. "Are you insane? Go even further into the charnel house?"

"Believe me, I'm not tremendously thrilled at the prospect either, Feldwebel. But the only way and I stress the *only* way out of here is to recapture the altar before the serpent lords torture Sweet Liesel and learn its secrets. Not only would that be a disaster of epic proportions, allowing them to control the appearance and disappearance of these pyramids at will, but it would also grant them the ability to subtly influence the war in ways we can only begin to guess at.

"There's also the fact that unless we retrieve the altar soon, Sweet Liesel's magics will expire and these ziggurats will sink back into the sands of their own accord, taking us with them. That will be followed by a long, painful eternity of servitude in the dark. Believe me I would rather have you shoot me, Feldwebel. It would be infinitely preferable to the alternative.

"Let me spell it out for you so there are no further misunderstandings: our best way out of here is to go deeper into the lair and retrieve that altar. It's not what I would choose in an ideal world, but there it is."

"And how do you plan to defeat a whole army of these serpent men? You said there were a multitude of these creatures?"

"Well that is an issue, but numbers alone are not always a guarantee of victory. I have one or two ideas that might prove useful... it's possible..."

"Ach, this is madness, madness, Herr Oberleutnant! Sneaking our way out? Well that I could possibly accept, but fighting a horde of these beasts? You see what they did to those SS? What they've done to those magicians? We won't last moments..."

"And what if they discover us in these tunnels? Better to return to the first chamber and make our defence there..."

Kurt and Jürgen continued to argue amongst themselves, while Captain Seraph looked on impassively. I must admit that both this place and the horrors we had encountered were making me doubt my judgement, but the captain was so candid, so convincing that I found it hard to be swayed against him— even by the arguments of my own men. In another moment the captain directed his gaze toward me and raising a quizzical eyebrow, said or perhaps seemed to say, for I swear his lips did not move.

You know I'm right. Trust me, this is our best, perhaps our only chance of leaving this place alive.

All I could do was nod.

"Gentlemen, gentlemen!" said the captain. "I believe your Oberleutnant wishes to speak."

"Kurt, Jürgen, I have heard what you have to say and while I value your advice, my instincts tell me we must trust this man and that is what I intend to do. We press on."

"But sir, if..."

"Silence Jürgen! The decision is made, or do you think the German *Heer* has suddenly become a democracy? Must I make this an order?"

Jürgen glowered, Kurt wavered and it was a grim moment, the terror of this place dissolving the bonds of discipline, comradeship to the point that I was almost compelled to reinforce my authority with my weapon. But then Captain Seraph interjected with a hissed 'listen gentlemen' and as he did, we heard it too, sounds beginning to seep into the chamber. It was nearly imperceptible at first, a low, sibilant moan, a repeated rhythmic insinuation like a hypnotic suggestion made flesh. It throbbed and pulsed seductively, seeming to be absorbed as much through the skin as through our ears. Vaguely I was aware of Little Hans scrabbling back down inside my pack.

But he was soon forgotten for although it was ineffably alien, to hear that sound was to be transported, entranced, ensorcelled, like Odysseus must have felt when he first heard the sirens' call. Our quarrel was forgotten, my weapon dropped numbly at my side and I, along with my comrades began to trudge mechanically towards the source of this bewitching aural beauty. Our brains became clouded, crowded, intoxicated by the most delightfully seductive coils, as our wills were subsumed to that all-powerful, all-encompassing melody.

"Caution gentlemen, not so fast," said Seraph, barring my progress with a surprisingly firm grip although I seemed to hear his voice from a thousand kilometres away. "The song of the snake is most alluring, but I'd rather you didn't fall completely under its spell." With that he reached into his jacket and took out an ankh-like talisman and hung it around my neck. See, I still wear it, even now and I do not think I will ever remove it.

The effect was extraordinary, for while I continued to hear the song, it immediately lost its hypnotic quality and my senses and my will gradually became my own again. Nimbly, Seraph placed one around Kurt's neck while I performed a similar manoeuvre on Jürgen and in a short time, we were all staring at each other rather sheepishly as I believe you British say.

"Don't worry gentlemen, you're not the first to fall under the snake's spell," said Captain Seraph. "But these charms should see you right."

"Ach, what was that?" asked Kurt, shaking his head ruefully. "Just like some of their lowly earth-bound cousins, certain of serpent kind have the ability to hypnotise their victims," said Captain Seraph. "In this case, they were able to seduce you by sound alone. Do not, if you value your lives or your sanity, remove those amulets, they will protect you from the spell's worst effects. Yet that otherworldly music would also seem to indicate that we are approaching our goal. Let's go cautiously from here on in gentlemen, for the wicket may about to become decidedly sticky." With that he strode off into the corridor moving quietly but decisively toward the haunting refrain which seemed to emanate from below us.

"Ach, the what may be about to become the *what*?" said Kurt.

"A British colloquial phrase, I think it means trouble ahead, if I understand correctly."

"Ach, I will never grasp their strange language, but what actually happened there? It was the most peculiar feeling, as if my will were no longer my own." Kurt shook his head. "How is it possible that mere music may rob a man's resolve?"

"I have no idea how or why, but let us say I will not be in a hurry to remove this charm he gave us. Without the captain's intervention I would have walked toward that sound – and most likely my doom – until the music stopped."

     Tomb of the Aeons

"I, too," said Jürgen. "Perhaps this *Engländer* may be worth heeding after all?"

So, following closely after Captain Seraph, we began our final descent into that pit of madness. Yes madness I say, for I will not lie to you, gentlemen. It is only with the profoundest effort I can recall the intimate details of what was to follow without my brain beginning to buckle and my precarious hold on sanity threatening to snap.

Down we crept and ever downward, the slow, steady throb of that bewitching music our constant companion, which in spite of our talisman's protection, still seemed to seep through flesh and penetrate our very bones. Closer now and ahead in the stygian gloom I began to see the glow of lights far along the passageways deep underground. Captain Seraph turned and motioned us to utter silence and now we slunk like the very shadows we had become, until we drew close to another great junction where many corridors and tunnels split off into the darkness.

Here another of those vile markers had been left. One of those lesser sorcerers hung upside down by his feet, his arms bound and his throat cut so that his life blood drained into a great brazen bowl, collecting there in a dark, viscous bubbling pool. Beyond was a vast portal, the stone shaped into the image of a vast serpent's jaws. A flickering crimson light danced beyond it, giving it the appearance of movement and animation, while all the while the music continued to throb and pulse. Quickly, we followed Captain Seraph as he waved us into cover in the lee of that loathsome sacrificial vessel.

Then abruptly in the middle of this precarious position, Captain Seraph seemed to fall into a reverie, his eyes wide and staring but vacant as if he were attempting to see beyond his immediate surrounds. Kurt and Jürgen were flattened against the wall behind me, but I, second in line, could see past both the captain and the great entranceway beyond. Long seconds, shallow breaths passed, but still the captain remained in his trance. Now the fantastic music seemed to grow in intensity and my eyes were riveted to that flickering square. Then a shadow detached itself from the gloom, a darker shape defined itself against the light and I saw him, the serpent man.

Oh, you may not believe me, dismiss these thoughts as the ramblings of a deranged, shell-shocked fool, but in my mind there is no doubt. For although the body was vaguely humanoid, that of a tall, angular man, his – its – head was all serpent: scaled skin, glowering, pitiless eyes fringed with a hood like a cobra's. It carried a cruel, sickle-like weapon and its tongue flickered, sampling the air as if seeking out prey. The sight was so bizarre, that my natural instincts bristled and I gripped my weapon. This creature triggered such feelings of revulsion that I knew I must kill it before it discovered us, for surely it would do likewise and without hesitation. Its gaze swept the corridor and surely now we must be discovered! The barrel of my weapon seemed to rise as if of its own accord, my finger tightened on the trigger...

But then a hand was on my arm and when I looked down it was Captain Seraph's. He smiled and my panic and terror seemed to drain away. For an instant I saw the remnants of a strange witch light play about his eyes but then that too faded and we were left alone in the gloom. When I looked again, the serpent man had gone, disappeared back towards whatever hellish rite was being played out in that chamber.

"Come," said the captain. "I believe I've found a way to approach our target unobserved."

As we retraced our steps, Captain Seraph suddenly darted into one of the labyrinth's many side passages quietly beckoning us to follow. We ascended a gently sloping set of stairs which led up onto a small landing. Leading off from this was a long gallery which was lit by the reflected glow of the red light below. Once again silently urging caution, Captain Seraph drew us to the edge of the stone lip where crouching, we had a good view of the vast space beneath.

This must surely be the heart of the creatures' nest for it was an immense oval chamber with huge curving walls which met far above our heads, dwarfing both ourselves and the assembly below. It reminded me of being trapped inside a giant, antediluvian egg, which now I think about it, would make perfect sense I suppose, for that is how their species enters this world. Inside this snake's womb, its inhuman architects had erected huge carved pillars and placed many bizarre idols to their serpent god. The whole space was lit by the flickering glow of flaming torches which gave off a cruel, yellow light adding an unreal, sinister filter to the scene.

Below, a congregation of countless snake men swayed and writhed to unholy rhythms and melodies while a portion of their number worked flute, drum and other instruments I could not even begin to name. Furthest away from us, where the gallery curved to the far wall, an enormous effigy, perhaps a hundred metres tall, dominated the scene, a truly colossal image of what can only have been their god, a revolting effigy of stone writ on a monumental scale, but so life-like that its scales seemed to shimmer and writhe in the orange-yellow half light. Great jewelled eyes glittered, infinitely old, infinitely evil and a hood like a cobra's spread a great shadow over its children who danced and writhed below. Lesser heads sprouted at irregular intervals from the main body of the idol and cascading, metre-thick coils fell to form a raised dais whereon a group of serpent men stood immobile.

It was a horrible yet strangely fascinating tableau and despite one's natural innate revulsion for those ophidian rites, it was not easy to peel one's eyes away from the mesmeric spectacle.

"It is Yig, or Father Set, the god of the serpent men," whispered Captain Seraph. "And see, the serpent lords there on the dais and if I am not mistaken, Fräulein Böhm too.» The captain must have eyes like an eagle›s, but a quick glance through my binoculars confirmed his assertion. Towering above their primitive subjects were indeed a group of formidably regal looking snake men, their sinewy bodies robed and adorned with all manner of brazen jewellery and ornaments in contrast to their semi-naked subjects.

At the back of the dais, the stone scales of the statue divided into a large, recessed alcove wherein a strange object blazed. This must surely be the Fangs of Set, the altar which the captain had spoken of earlier, for it was an object formed of unlikely angles, slithering coils and strange intersections which had an unwholesome look to it and which seemed to have no place in the natural order of this world. At its heart, a sinister red light pulsed, a strobing palpitation which cut through the shadows, lending the scene a kind of stop-motion quality which confused one's senses.

Yet despite this incredible sight, the thing which most readily attracted my eye was the one human figure on that stage. To the front a forked cross had been erected and bound to it was a small, slender woman in the tattered remains of an SS Obersturmführer 's uniform. Her head lolled forward on her chest as if from fatigue or pain and long, dark red hair fell over her shoulders. Her half naked body bore multiple wounds as if her flesh had been cut precisely but shallowly many times, and blood flowed darkly down her arms from hands which had been nailed directly to the wood. Even in the midst of that unearthly horror, it was a most pitiable sight and I whispered to the captain.

"What must we do?"

"Any intervention now would be absolute suicide. Patience, Herr Oberleutnant, we must bide our time and hope circumstances afford us an opportunity. In the meantime, let's move a little closer and observe."

Shielded by the mantle we worked our way along the gallery while the hypnotic sounds and insistent rhythms continued to beat out from below. Soon, we had scuttled along the entire length of the walkway and found ourselves concealed within the shadows of the coils of the great serpent itself. There, we had a prime overview as some twenty metres below we could see the serpent lords' horribly detailed inhuman visages as they received the foul, unbridled worship of their countless followers, row upon row of lidless eyes shining in horrible unison as they paid obeisance.

"While they are occupied, we had best make use of this opportunity," whispered Captain Seraph. "Pass me those bags if you'd be so kind, Feldwebel."

After Kurt had complied, we kept watch while the captain busied himself, but now the music began to build to a crescendo and the snake men became more animated as they jigged and cavorted to the bewitching sound. I sensed things may be about to come to a climax and I think Captain Seraph did too for now he finished off his preparations and gave the stage his fullest attention.

One of the snake lords, the python-headed one, strode over to the woman on the cross and raised her head toward the assembly. Even from above I could see her eyeballs had rolled back into her head and just the pale whites were showing and for one horrible moment I thought he meant to strike off her head. Then abruptly, as if at some pre-arranged signal, the music cut out and the python lord's voice rang out in a single long word which washed and swam around that great dome, echoing and re-echoing in a way which no human mouth could or should try to articulate. Then he let her head go and it flopped back against her chest and the great horde quietly turned and began to file out through the entranceways, soon to be followed by their masters. But why and for what purpose I could not fathom.

"I have little idea either," whispered the captain. "That ancient word he intoned meant 'prepare' I think. But prepare for what? We had best seize our chance, it shouldn't be too hard to work our way down. The statue's coils may look ominous, but they'll provide good foot holds. Come on."

With that he flung himself over the side and, displaying a considerable agility, began to swarm down the scales of the snake, wire trailing behind him. Kurt and Jürgen looked at me for guidance, but I merely shrugged. After all we had heard and seen, it seemed entirely natural we should place ourselves in his hands. I believe you British even have a phrase for it, no? *In for a penny, in for a pound.*

In this, as in those other matters he had described, Captain Seraph was proved right and it was with little difficulty the three of us began our climb down. The altar continued to pulse and glow evilly but as we negotiated the last couple of metres, the captain was already at the Saltire as he termed that wooden cross, placing his fingers at the neck of the woman. Even as he felt for a pulse I could see she was in a bad way, her body cut and bleeding, streams of blood flowing almost unnaturally slowly down from her palms. Even to my untutored eye, it looked as if she would not survive for long. Captain Seraph urged me over and said quietly.

"Take her weight, this won't be pleasant."

Nodding, I held her slight frame while the captain produced what looked like a curved set of pliers from inside his jacket. Grasping one arm by the wrist, he took hold of the head of the nail and strained, his face contorting as he pulled it through both wood and palm sending out sprays of arterial blood. It was grim work and I dared not look again as the metal slid through flesh with an appalling sucking sound. Unsupported, her body sagged and it was as well that she was insentient, for she would have screamed in agonies had she been conscious. Quickly and efficiently, the captain repeated the procedure on the other hand

and then cut the cords which bound her legs. I laid her down gently, but our efforts were surely wasted, for her face was as white as bleached bone and freed from the cross, her wounds suddenly bled profusely, staining the dais crimson.

Captain Seraph knelt down beside her and one hand on her brow and the other clutching a peculiar looking totem, he began mumbling beneath his breath. The words weren't in any language I recognised, but seemed to consist of almost musically sung phrases, although I believe I heard a single recognisable word which sounded like 'Imhotep'. Then, perhaps it was just a trick of the light, but a silver-white glow seemed to suffuse both the amulet and his features and slowly began to transfer itself through his body. Gradually this aura crept the length of his arm and when it touched her face, her whole body gave a great shudder, arching and stiffening and her head jerked back as the light flowed over her skin and seemed to engulf her. It went on to immerse her whole body and then she let out a great long sigh, like the sound of wind through the trees and relaxed, went limp, wilting, as he lowered her onto the ground.

The radiance flowed through her and then drained away and now her wounds were gone and her flesh began to bloom again like yours or mine. It was quite simply one of the most extraordinary things I have ever seen, but when I turned to question Captain Seraph, it was he who appeared to be pale and trembling, as if he had undergone some terrible ordeal.

"Don't worry, Herr Oberleutnant, I will be quite restored in a short while."

"But... what... how?"

"Just a little something I picked up on my travels. Don't tell the Red Cross though, I'm not sure they'd approve. Ah, it appears the Fräulein is regaining consciousness. "

He spoke the truth and already her eyes were opening and she blinked, breathing deeply. All at once her features which had a certain youthful sweetness in repose, hardened like smelted steel and seeing my face looming over her, she barked,

"Oberleutnant. Where am I? What's happened? Report!"

"Relax, Liesel. You're safe, at least for now," said the captain, finally shaking off the after effects of his intervention.

"Seraph! I might have known. Oberleutnant, shoot this man immediately!"

"Well charming, I must say," drawled the captain, "And delightful to see you too my dear Sweet Liesel. Remind me, what happened to preserving your most valuable assets?"

"Do not refer to me by the odious name. Oberleutnant, your weapon now!"

I hesitated, not knowing how to respond, especially given the events of the past few moments. But this seemed to infuriate her.

"Oberleutnant, you see these rank badges on what remains of my uniform? Have you forgotten your duty to the Fatherland?"

"I ... that is, I have not Fräulein, but..."

"You will address me as Obersturmführer!"

"Now don't bully the poor Oberleutnant into doing anything hasty, Liesel, at least until I have brought you up to speed on current events."

"Don't patronise me, Seraph..."

"Not patronage, survival and believe me you are going to need all my help in extricating yourself from the pretty pickle you find yourself in. So put aside your anger for a moment and just listen..."

Liesel Böhm 's brown eyes blazed with contempt as Captain Seraph began to describe the events which had drawn us here, but slowly, understanding dawned and she became calmer, listening intently, especially to the last portion of the tale which the captain glossed over by simply stating he had revived her. When he was done, she asked,

"Is this true, Oberleutnant?"

"Yes Fräu ... Obersturmführer as far as I can tell. Yet the captain hardly gives himself enough credit. When we discovered you, you were not just wounded, but fatally so, or so it appeared to me. How he bought you back from the brink of death I still do not know, but it was truly remarkable."

While she examined the scars on her palms, I briefly outlined the circumstances which had brought my men here.

"Hm, I see. Captain Seraph is evidently a man of many talents," she said, eyeing him thoughtfully and with perhaps slightly less hostility than before. The captain responded with an incline of his head.

"My talents, meagre as they are, are probably best discussed another time. What concerns me... what concerns us all now, is how we are to retrieve the Fangs of Set and flee this place without further incurring the wrath of the serpent lords. Any thoughts Swe... Obersturmführer?"

"What of my sorcerers?"

"Truth to tell they met a rather sticky end. They are currently doing duty as inverted signposts on the way down. We won't be able to count on their help."

"Well, you evidently found your way in here, surely we can just retrace your steps, evade the snake men and find our way back to the surface?"

"Interesting idea, but we can't leave the Fangs of Set in the serpent men's coils. If they master its powers – and I've no doubt they will – then it means the war in North Africa becomes infinitely more complex. They'll be able to rematerialize this place at will, awaken the other sleeping serpent metropolises… affect the course of the conflict in ways we can only begin to imagine. It would have been better if you had not meddled with them or brought the artefact to this place at all…"

"Meddled? I? The plan was sound, we could not have anticipated…"

"Anticipated? I hardly believe becoming the *amuse bouche* in a snake lord's sacrifice was what you anticipated? Or is the Fatherland's mission evaluation operating on different criteria these days?"

"It was worth the risk, with the knowledge these creatures possess…"

"Oh yes, their knowledge. I rather suspect I know what you would have used that 'knowledge' for…"

"And what of it? Eichmann is doing remarkable work…"

"Genocide is remarkable, but not in the way you mean. I wonder, if you would feel the same way when the serpent men turn their attentions toward your beloved Reich? We will see how remarkable it feels then. You think you can tame *them* with your petty magics? Of all the foolish, ignorant, misguided…"

"Captain, Obersturmführer..." I tried to gain their attention but their blood was rising.

"...And what would you know about dealing with *Untermenschen*? You and your pathetic British sense of fair play? Parasites must be eradicated, not tolerated."

"Eradicated? A fancy word for cold-blooded slaughter, and no man or woman is worth less than any other."

"You lack the will to recognise what must be done."

" Obersturmführer! Captain! This is not the time..."

"How dare you interrupt, Oberleutnant! Give me your weapon. To think I was foolish indeed to entertain the thought of an alliance with this implacable enemy of the Fatherland!"

"Obersturmführer, the serpent men, they are returning! Listen." They both turned and sure enough, now they were no longer hurling insults at each other, they perceived the noise that had alerted me.

The tread of many feet approached, lights flickered in the entrance-ways and licked around the doors, heralding the return of our foe. Quickly I signalled Jürgen and Kurt to take up defensive positions behind the altar where the alcove provided a degree of natural cover.

"Well, it seems the decision is made for us," said the captain as he and the Obersturmführer scrambled in beside us. I hefted the Black Sun weapon up to my shoulder and sighted down the barrel. Despite the strange, *futuristischen* design, it felt reassuring and weighty. It would need to be. "Orders?" I asked.

"Hold fire..." they said simultaneously and the look she directed at him was positively venomous.

"With the Obersturmführer's permission of course..." said Captain Seraph, "Let them make the first move. But if they turn hostile, don't hesitate or it will be our lives."

We waited while the slow tread of the serpent legions descended and as the tension mounted, I could feel sweat bead across my forehead, my muscles tightening as that dread sound approached. We did not have long to wait, for the first of the creatures now began to stream through the entranceways, filing in like automatons to take up their positions in front of their great graven idol.

One of them must have spotted the tenantless cross and with a sharp cry and pointed arm, alerted the rest of its fellows to our poorly concealed presence. The foremost of them then came on in a great surge and I was just about to shout the order, when the captain did it for me. *"Feuer eröffnen!"*

Mein Gott but those Black Sun assault rifles were something, experimental weapons of great power and extreme ferocity. Our initial salvo carved great gaping rents in their ranks, serpent men falling, bleeding and dying under our withering fire. Not one made it onto the raised portion of the dais, which formed our platform and in less than twenty seconds under the controlled power of those scything bursts, they were put to flight, streaming back in headlong retreat, shrieking and crying in that strange otherworldly tongue of theirs. All that was left was the moans of the wounded and dying.

Despite the apparent hopelessness of our situation, I returned Kurt and Jürgen's grins as we surveyed the havoc we had wrought.

"Round one to us then," said the captain, "But they'll be back for more. Keep your eyes open, while I finish wiring this up." Several minutes passed, but despite torchlight continuing to flicker beyond the entranceway, not a single snake man showed himself. Captain Seraph was finishing up his work when a sibilant voice cut through the air.

"Humansss!" The voice was in our language but that single word contained as much contempt and hatred as I have ever heard expressed. It rang and reverberated around the great dome, seeming to whisper from everywhere at once.

"Who is brave enough to dare disturb the tomb of the serpent lords? Speak, for we sense the presssence of a great sssorcerer amongst you."

"I am Liesel..." said the Obersturmführer, starting to rise.

"Not you female, we know what you are. Who is this other? Speak, for we would know your name human."

"Oh pardon me, is my aura showing? Modesty forbids," said Captain Seraph. "I have been called many things, many names, all you need know is that you face a servant of the light."

"A bold servant indeed to walk our hallsss, penetrate our holy sanctum, unbidden, unasssked, uninvited."

"True, yet my presence is not of my own choosing, I was held captive earlier and well, this is the first opportunity I've had to properly introduce myself."

"Do not mock us, for we know what you truly are *Astari*, though not how you managed to conceal yourself amongst these mortals. Now, before I waste any more of my people's lives in subduing you, tell usss what is it you intend? Perhaps a compromissse might be reached?"

"Perhaps it might," said the captain. "I have no quarrel with you snake lord or your people, but I cannot allow you to retain the altar. What I suggest is that you allow myself and my companions to leave this place with the altar intact and no further harm will come to either side."

"Allow? Retain? Audaciousss words when you nestle in the very bosom of Father Yig. This foolish female merely returned to us that which has belonged to my people down the long aeonsss. It is ours by right."

"Well, that is a matter for debate, however you do make a compelling point and in the normal course of events one I would naturally concede gracefully," said the captain. "Nevertheless, I must remain firm on this issue. If you truly know who and what I am, you will heed my words and save us all a lot of suffering."

"Tell me sorcerer, if the posssitions were reversed would you allow me to walk out of your home with one of your greatest lost treasuresss?"

"No, no, I don't believe I would and when you put it like that it doesn't seem very fair does it? But I'm afraid I must insist. If you attempt to recover the artefact by force, I will destroy it and bring this temple down around your ears. Do not doubt it. "

"Doubt it we do not, *Astari,* you are a worthy foe, but like you, the Serpent lords are uncomprimisssing."

With that last hissed syllable all hell seemed to break loose. Suddenly the galleries on both sides above us were alive with snake men and a hail of spears and darts rained down. Some, no doubt close relatives of their terrestrial cousins, spat balls of venom which splashed close by, causing the stone to burn and smoke with an acidic poison. A javelin grazed me, causing a hot streak of pain along my cheek and then I was firing, raking the galleries and shouting at Kurt and Jürgen to do likewise. I saw Captain Seraph take a hit of venom to the chest and the impact spun him like a scarecrow in a hurricane and he seemed to fall in slow motion. There was a cry of anguish from behind me, Kurt or Jürgen I could not tell, and then there was no time for thought as I was firing, firing desperately to stem the serpent tide.

Our guns barked and smoked, heavy calibre bullets biting and rending, scything down snake men by the score. Yet for every one that fell, a dozen more seemed to spring up to take his place. In between our volleys they popped up with little regard for their own safety to unleash missile or venom and with the advantage of both high ground and cover now too, their advantage was growing. It might be moments, it might be seconds but surely it could not be long before they overwhelmed us and we must succumb to their brutal mercies? I glanced behind me. Captain Seraph was still down and Jürgen was staring numbly at the spear which had transfixed his thigh.

"Obersturmführer ? Orders? What must we do?"

"Keep firing! Kill them all." she yelled having taken up the fallen Jürgen's assault rifle and was now adding her own deadly skills to our firepower. "If all fails, save a bullet for yourself. Believe me, you do not want to be taken alive. If we must die, let us die like true *Deutsches Volk*."

"Oh I think we can do a little better than that," whispered Captain Seraph, staggering groggily back to his feet. The venom had blasted and melted the front of his jacket so that his pale flesh showed through.

"The time for compromise is over. They can't say I didn't warn them, you all heard me. Huddle into the alcove and take cover. This is about to get very messy." As we scrambled for safety, the captain took a second and then very deliberately depressed the plunger.

A moment later and the very earth itself spasmed and shook. The charges Captain Seraph had carefully rigged around the statue detonated with a devastating effect and I saw the gallery above us thrown wildly through the air, disintegrating as it spewed snake men screaming to their deaths. Rock, dust and stone were thrown down upon us and careered about the vast chamber adding to the confusion and then, from far above, there came an ominous creaking, rending sound, as if a colossus groaned.

"Down! Down!" shouted Seraph as a great crack rent the air and the graven image of the giant serpent god lurched away from its supports. I looked up along the length of the coils as it tilted in what seemed like slow motion, shedding rock and stone. Then it reached a tipping point and accelerated, smashed like a drunken titan against the outer wall. I had just time to close my eyes and curse and then the very heavens themselves seemed to fall in a choking miasma of cloying powder and dust.

CHAPTER FIVE: THE DANCE OF THE PILLARS

There was a short, dark, timeless space where I think I may have lost consciousness, for I remember nothing. Then I was dimly aware of something rubbing against my nose, butting my cheek and meowing pitiably. I subsided weakly, but then it was licking my face, a rough sandpapery tongue which prompted a fit of coughing and spluttering as I struggled to draw breath into my desiccated lungs. When the fit had passed, I opened dust-crusted eyes and there was Little Hans, perched on my chest, regarding me curiously in that way that only cats have.

"Delightful little fellow, sorry to scare you like that." said Captain Seraph, scooping up Little Hans and nuzzling him against his cheek. The cat responded by purring deeply and inclining its head against the captain's chin, evidently in flights of ecstasy. "Well, hello to you too little chap," he said, contemplating the feline with real affection. "I'm inordinately fond of our feline friends, you know, Herr Oberleutnant," he said, helping me to my feet, "And this one's quite the little prince, aren't you?"

"Ach, Little Hans is the true commander of our panzer," I grinned and leaning for support against the wall, I surveyed what remained of our party. The altar's strange angles and weird geometry continued to pulse a sombre crimson and while Kurt was gradually picking himself up, the Obersturmführer attempted to brush the dust and debris from the remains of her uniform. Jürgen lay still, though whether from his wound or some glancing blow from the fallen masonry, I could not tell.

Beyond the confines of our shelter, fierce swirls and eddies began to settle in the main chamber. I could see the outline of a heap of rubble which had been deposited on the smooth open floor and the partial remains of columns which had tumbled to the ground. There, measured out along its length, the weight of the snake god's statue had rent a great tear in the outer wall, which now lay open to the stars. Already, I could see the first streaks of dawn were beginning to colour the horizon and despite our sorry state, I began to taste real hope that we would succeed in escaping this foul place.

"A bold strategy Captain Seraph," said the Obersturmführer. "But I salute you for it. Desperate times call for radical solutions."

"Not a maxim I would care to live by and I rather think this little affair may not be entirely over quite yet. So let's not count our chickens."

"Count our what?"

"*Sich nicht um ungelegte Eier kümmern, Fräulein.* Don't count your eggs before they are hatched."

As if on cue, a deep sonorous voice rang out from beyond the confines of the entranceways. Although the words were in German, the serpentine accent enunciated them carefully, seething and boiling with a scarcely contained fury. Its tone chilled me to the very marrow.

"Foul human cattle! Hereticsss! Dessspoilers! Uninvited you sssummoned us, disturbing our ancient rest, interrupting our dreams of eternity, drawing us once again to the surface lands against our will.

"Godlesss infidels! We did not ask for this. You, you have invaded our sssanctuary, despoiled it with your pessstilential presence, fouled the ancient paths where no human foot has trod for millennia!

"You taunt us by returning one of our great treasuresss, threaten us with your feeble insssinuations, attempt to cozen us with your petty schemes of glory and power.

"Now you have defiled the inner temple of Yig, destroyed the most holy of holies, the sssanctuary of he who is oldest and darkessst, who had dominion over this world when mankind, a mewling infant, was still crawling on its belly.

"Woe to you, woe to you *Astari*, for you have ignited the wrath of the serpent lords. Now you and your companions will not die as mortal men, but live and suffer for as long as we endure.

"You will beg for death, urge usss for it, plead for its sssweet release. But it will not come. Oh we will make sure to preserve your mind, not allow you the comfort of insanity, ssso you may know the dissscipline of pain and fully comprehend it every moment for all eternity. Behold, for the Spawn of Yig approaches and your doom is now sealed!"

Beyond the rubble, beyond the lighted archways something indeed began to stir and out in that space, the lights began to go out, one by one, melting away as the torches were extinguished or withdrawn. There was a commotion which for some reason reminded me of mice scattering before the approach of a feared predator and soon, just the strobing pulses of that accursed altar were our only illumination. A strange, queasy, oleaginous kind of silence gripped the chamber and now the very stars themselves seemed to look down upon us, their breath held, for who or whatever lay out there beyond the range of our senses.

"What is it? What have they called forth?" said the Obersturm-führer and it was the first time I had heard even a hint of doubt colour her voice.

"I don't dare imagine," said Captain Seraph. "But I doubt it's here to serve us cocktails. Do what you can to prepare yourselves and try not to look upon it directly for too long, whatever it is. For that way madness and death undoubtedly lies."

His words echoed out to be swallowed by the depths of the cavern. That same vast quietude seemed to descend upon the whole place and although we could hear nothing, one could sense the impending doom approaching us.

This feeling of ancient, awe-inspiring dread built until I could take no more and wished to scream for release. But then a wave of darkness seemed to slink into the chamber like a tangible thing. It crept and wound itself around the remaining pillars, shedding wisps and shreds of a pure inky blackness that seemed the very negative of life force.

The cloud insinuated itself along the floor, hugging the flagged stone like the serpents which had summoned it, mounting and swarming up over the rubble until it reached the zenith of the debris. There it seemed to gather in upon itself, forming a great irregular tower of darkness, which span and gyrated with chaotic fury, forming and reforming itself, throwing out dark arms, spokes, membranous limbs, swirling with myriad unholy shapes. The sight threatened my increasingly fragile grip on sanity and yet when I tried to look away I could not. Then its darkling shroud seemed to rend and tear and fall away and we were left regarding the loathsome beast which materialised before us.

Well had the serpent lords named it, for this Spawn of Yig was a foul creature which should never have walked upon this Earth or any other. Its form seemed to twist and meld before our eyes and then, fluidly, it resolved itself into the shape of a gigantic snake demon, its body coils glistening with darkling scales that dripped a shadowy gelatinous ichor. But where a mortal snake had but a single head, this creature sported many, six main ones, each framed in the form of its corresponding snake species. Further offshoots and tendrils hung from its body like unwholesome fruit and it gave off a foul, pestilential odour as its myriad heads balefully swept around the chamber seeking its prey.

"*Mein Gott,*" I heard Kurt exclaim and my hands shook, as I tried to press a fresh magazine into my weapon.

"How do we fight *that*?"

"You don't," said Captain Seraph. "Or rather, you don't directly. Leave that to me. But I need a little time to prepare, can you buy me some?"

"I..." words would not come as I eyed the foul horror of the creature, almost transfixed by the sheer alien wrongness of it.

"I just need you to distract it. It's powerful and deadly, yes, but not exactly mobile. See, it won't be able to catch you amongst the columns if you're quick. I won't need long, a couple of minutes at most, just keep it away from us and this altar," he said, clutching Little Hans and eyeing the Obersturmführer meaningfully.

I can't have replied for I was still dumbstruck by the sight of the demon. But then Captain Seraph took hold of my shoulders, shook me and his eyes blazed into mine.

"You must do this, it is our only hope. Quickly now, let's be about it, bullets won't harm it, only most likely annoy the hell out of it, so be as trigger happy as you like. Noise, movement, shouting, anything. Get its attention and once it has your scent, run like the wind. Keep to the pillars and keep turning as much as possible, it'll find it difficult to manoeuvre in there." Those eyes, those words seemed to trigger something within me and I began to feel my courage return.

"Kurt, with me, now!" I shouted and as the captain dragged the Obersturmführer to the altar and placed Little Hans upon it, I threw caution to the winds and leapt into the shattered arena to confront the beast, before fear could return and change my mind.

Kurt dropped down beside me and we scuttled for the shelter of the nearest column and stood apparently unobserved. Perhaps the creature's eyesight wasn't very powerful?

"Hunting the enemy's big guns, just like the good old days," said Kurt but his attempt at humour was as thin as a spring frost.

"Not any good old days I remember," I replied and in that moment, I knew I must do the deed now and provoke it before my courage evaporated again. I nodded and ducked around the column, waving and shouted.

"Hey!" A couple of the beast's tendrils flapped, seeming to regard me, but its main heads had caught sight of Captain Seraph and the Obersturmführer who had joined hands over the altar and begun chanting a strange incantation upon it.

I remember thinking strangely 'this will not do at all', an absurdly facile objection in the face of such supernatural terror and shouldering my rifle, I unleashed a burst of fire which slammed into the creature's heads and body. Kurt added his fire to my own and our bullets sliced into the demon, raking its flesh and causing a foul ichor to drip from those newly made lesions.

Every head and limb of that foul excrescence turned at once in our direction and it gave a terrifying, nerve-shredding roar, which I am not ashamed to say caused my stomach to clench. In an instant the beast had turned its full attention upon us, hissing and spitting it began to writhe loathsomely toward us, coils tumbling over each other in a foul disjointed motion, as it latched onto the scent of a new prey: us.

So began a deadly game of cat and mouse, as I believe you British say, an expression which was to prove oddly prophetic.

Kurt and I fell back before the beast's advance, dodging behind pillars to shield ourselves from its pursuit and sprinting from column to column, cover to cover. Yet always it pursued us, relentless, determined, full of hate and yearning to crush and rend the insects which had stung it so sorely. Its hot breath was a constant on our backs and while the demon was powerful, it was not overly intelligent and we could use our cunning and guile to deceive it. As the captain had observed the narrow spaces between the columns was our greatest ally and the bulk of its body also worked against it there, while our nimbler forms allowed us to dash, turn and double back, evading its pursuit.

Yet it was still a desperate business and I knew we could not escape the creature forever as the sheer physical effort required to stay one step ahead of it was immense.

Some of its heads were venomous and when it paused, they spat balls of an acidic poison which fizzled and hissed as they cut into the stone where moments before we had been. Remorselessly, it hunted us and on a nodded signal to Kurt, we split apart, hoping to divide its attention further. While its focus was on me, Kurt fired another burst which caused it to lumber off in pursuit of him and I had a brief moment to observe our companions on the dais.

Captain Seraph and Obersturmführer Böhm were bathed in a nimbus of golden light which extended out from the altar and if I was not mistaken, that was Little Hans at the centre of it, suspended about half a metre above its surface, while the captain inscribed strange patterns which lingered in the air. Whatever they were up to, I had no time to question it, for our situation was now becoming truly desperate.

"Captain, Obersturmführer!" I shouted, but they did not seem to hear me and as I turned, I suddenly had problems enough of my own. Distracted, I had lost track of the demon and now it had closed in upon me, its sinister bulk looming on either side of the column where I had hidden. One of the smaller heads whipped through the air, striking at me and I had just enough wit to duck away from its fangs. But in evading its attack I had unwittingly backed against a gigantic slab of fallen stone. Almost immediately, one of its tendrils twisted around my leg, while another, razor sharp, burst through my left shoulder pinioning me. I gave a cry, for the pain was excruciating and dropping my weapon, I tried to tear away the demon limb with my hands. It was little use, for the tendril was like a steel hawser and I could not shift it one centimetre.

One by one each of the snake heads materialised around the column and as I groped for the hand grenade at my belt, I hoped my end would come swiftly, determined that my last thoughts should be of my wife and our last Bavarian spring together.

Now the creature's heads hovered over me, eyes narrowing as it triumphantly regarded its prone victim. Manifold fangs were bared, glistening, and then slowly, as if prolonging the agony, the heads all drew back in unison, ready to strike. With my last remaining strength, I grasped the pin of the *Stielhandgranate*, hoping that the explosion would not only consume me but might damage the creature where our bullets had failed. Staring into that bank of cruel, ophidian eyes, I pulled the pin, steeled myself to wait, wait for the bite, wait for the fangs to pierce my flesh and then, only then, in my death agonies would I trigger the explosive.

I was so transfixed by those lidless eyes that I was barely aware of a blur of movement to one side. In that instant I watched them transform from predatory hunter to furious victim as one, they reared and drew back from me in mortal agony.

Kurt! It was Kurt, who having seen the danger I was in and in one of the bravest acts I have ever witnessed, had fixed a bayonet and simply charged the creature. How he summoned the courage to perform such an act I will never know, but so intent was the demon on its prey, it had neglected its other quarry. Now it paid for this presumption, for Kurt had transfixed it, thrusting the blade through the eye socket of the python head and pulling the assault rifle's trigger, so that he emptied the entire magazine into its brain in an act of marvellous, desperate courage.

Thrashing, the demon shook and spasmed and I fell limp, almost helpless as the tendrils withdrew, snaking quickly back to their host.

The python head hung flaccid and lifeless, flopping pathetically against the floor, but in saving me, Kurt had doomed himself. Now its tendrils struck again, piercing and wrapping around his body, lifting that brave old soldier up until he dangled metres above the floor. This time its heads struck without hesitation, rising and falling in quick succession and their poison coursed through his body so that it swelled and bubbled until the veins burst and overflowed in a crimson arc. His death cry was strangled in his throat and then the demon tore him apart and discarded the lifeless husk like the shell of a cracked walnut.

Now in unison the heads turned my way again and while half of their number fixed me with a baleful gaze, the other half looked beyond toward the dais. Back in the entranceways, I could see the serpent men begin to mass again, gathering behind their demon-champion, presumably eager to watch the deaths of the invaders who had defied them.

Now I knew that our doom was truly and finally upon us, for I was weak as a newborn and could scarcely muster enough strength to stand, let alone continue that deadly game of hide and seek. I clutched the grenade and gathered it to me, ready to sell my life dearly as the demon turned toward me again.

I glanced at where Captain Seraph and the Obersturmführer had stood, but now the dais was emitting a brilliant, golden light which pierced that huge chamber. It bathed the demon in a blinding nimbus and the creature shrank away, retreating from the glare as if scalded. Momentarily it was as if a living star had been summoned into the chamber and instinctively I averted my gaze from the dazzling light. Then it was gone, fading away, diminishing as if it had never been.

In its place was the most extraordinary being. Its form was that of a woman, though one grown to a remarkable size for she stood perhaps five metres tall. Her shapely body was wrapped in pure white Egyptian linen, trimmed with gold and black and decorated with gleaming hieroglyphs which seemed to generate a golden aura which shimmered over her entire body. She was clad in the richest jewellery and in her hands, which were clasped across her chest, she held both a symbol I recognised as an Ankh and a strange rattle-like instrument which I have since learned is called a sistrum.

All this would no doubt be remarkable enough, for one does not expect to see giant glowing women appear from the ether. Strangest of all though, where one would have expected to see a celestial face to match the vision below, the head of what I can only describe as a lioness topped those shoulders, its eyes closed.

For a second nothing moved, nothing breathed and I was simply too stunned to comprehend what I saw.

But then the Spawn of Yig, evidently regarding this new arrival too and not liking it one bit, spat its defiance toward the interloper. Those eyes opened, golden cat's eyes which shone coolly, menacingly, as they perceived the snake demon. From behind the creature I heard a collective hiss escape from the serpent men, as if they recognised and feared this new foe. Then the giant feline-woman took a nonchalant step forward from the dais and now I could see cats, hundreds, perhaps thousands of the creatures, surrounding her, a furry horde which played about her feet.

With a grace which was undisputedly feline the entity padded forward, extending its arm, shaking the sistrum in rhythmic strokes which were at once melodious and percussive yet also daunting and sinister. With her came her attendant court of cats, swarming and circling around her great feet, a furry, chaotic cloud of bright eyes, swishing tails and arching fury. The attendant serpent men quailed at the sound and the advance of the feline horde, but the Spawn of Yig hissed its contempt and ignoring me, slithered forward to meet this new challenge. The two fabulous combatants met in the middle of that great ruined chamber, renewing an ancient conflict which had not been fought in centuries.

The two weighed each other up. The Spawn of Yig's heads and tendrils swayed as if seeking an opening, but the cat creature was quite still, quiet, perfectly balanced, except where once giant human hands had grasped sistrum and ankh, now emerged the gigantic paws and claws of a lioness.

She eyed the Spawn of Yig perfectly equitably, as if unperturbed by its menacing display and then her claws slid silently out just as the snake struck! The movement was almost too quick for the human eye to follow, but the response was like quicksilver and in an instant, the feline was no longer there, evading the snake demon's attack artfully and the serpent's fangs and tendrils snapped at empty air. Yet even though there had seemed to be no perceptible movement, when the Spawn of Yig retreated, another of its heads now fell limp and shredded to the floor, a razor claw had rent the cobra's hood!

So they danced in the strange, inhuman battle, for how long I do not know for now it seems so unreal, so surreal, that it took on a dream-like quality and I can scarcely believe I witnessed such a primordial encounter at all. Their movements, the attacks, thrusts, parries and counters were so deft they were almost beyond the perception of human senses. Such was their speed, ferocity and yes, grace, I do not believe such a sight was ever meant to be witnessed by mortal eyes at all.

The snake demon snarled and hissed and spat and yet for all its fury, it could not lay a single blow upon the cat goddess. However fast it struck, the feline was always faster, no matter how it twisted and contorted, the cat was more agile and however much it spat its hate, the greater was the feline's indifference as it shifted its weight and balanced with its great tawny tail.

More and more wounds marked the Spawn of Yig's body, its tendrils neatly and cruelly severed, one by one its heads fastidiously mauled so that soon it was the Spawn of Yig which was forced to retreat and evade the feline's languid attacks.

Little good it did though, for the feline struck with the precision of a surgeon, dissecting, cutting, severing with the most precise strokes and the most supreme nonchalance. Soon, just two heads remained on the Spawn of Yig, ichor spilled from multiple wounds and all of its demon tendrils lay severed, wriggling impotently upon the ground.

Now it backed away as the great cat stalked remorselessly forward. Desperate, helpless, its twin heads wove and hissed with impotent rage until its coils met the outer wall and then there was nowhere left to retreat. The feline's tail shivered furiously for an instant and then it sprang, a fury of teeth and claws, tearing, shredding the serpent demon which fell before its savage assault.

A great groan rent the air, as the snake men watched their champion die and this seemed to act as a signal to the feline's attendant brood, which now charged toward the entranceways. The stream of cats was a biting, clawing cloud of spite and the serpent men fled before it, flinging their weapons away and running headlong back through the tunnels with the felines following in close pursuit.

A great silence filled the chamber as the sound of the snake men's headlong retreat echoed in the warren. Then the cat creature turned from its grisly kill and once again unfurled itself until it stood upright. With large eyes unblinking, it began slowly and methodically to rasp a rough tongue across its ichor-stained paws. It saw me and for a moment its head inclined slightly in that way that cats have, when they are simply curious or perhaps deciding upon the merits of a further, easily digestible morsel.

"Gracious Bastet, goddess-empress of the noble race of felines. We, your friends and allies, thank you for your intervention."

It was Captain Seraph of course, who had delicately interposed himself between my shattered frame and the towering creature.

"Yet know," continued the captain in a melodious voice which was almost a song, "Your work on this plane is now done. Return now, return to the sleeping gardens, return to the dreaming throne, knowing that the day is won and your enemy is vanquished."

The creature's tawny golden eyes regarded the captain and for a moment a hint of annoyance, of thwarted caprice seemed to play across its features, but then it inclined its head in a nod of acknowledgement. Its massive form began to shrink, its body growing smaller and smaller, the nimbus of light retracting until it had diminished down to an almost human size. The feline features seemed to linger in the air and then with a last swish of its fading tail, they too were gone and a pair of bodies crumpled to the floor.

One was the mewling form of Little Hans, who extended his paws to land with ease and then, tail high like a mast, sauntered toward me to investigate my sorry state. The other was Liesel Böhm but she simply collapsed, falling to the ground with an indelicate thud, seemingly unconscious. While Little Hans nudged and bumped against me, the captain quickly checked the fallen Obersturmführer and once he was done, came and sat beside me.

"Lie a moment, let me have a look at you." Captain Seraph's hands ran up and down my body hovering over the flesh without ever touching it. He paused where the demon's tendrils had gripped my leg which was now a mass of dark, bruised welts, then at my shoulder, which the tendril had actually pierced. The shoulder burned intensely and dripped a dark, foul liquid. Looking at it I believe I had received my death wound.

"Nasty, but don't worry, it's salvageable, we won't be burying you quite yet. Stay still for a moment and let me concentrate."

That pale glow seemed to emanate from his palms once again and when he held them to the wound, a cool, soothing sensation permeated my shoulder, as if an angel were gently caressing it. I almost cried out with the intense sense of relief and my shoulder seemed to spontaneously heal itself under the captain's ministrations, the ichor drying up, the flesh renewing and resealing itself. He repeated the procedure with my leg until it too had knit together and just pale puckered flesh remained.

"Rest for a few moments. Don't try to move, this has been quite an ordeal."

"Ordeal? I scarcely know where to begin, Captain." I said, carefully reinserting the pin back into the live grenade.

"Then don't, this incident has already taken us to many dark places, there seems little sense in delving even further. Naturally, I will do what I can to answer any remaining questions you have. I'm sorry about your crew, your friend was a brave fellow to sacrifice himself like that."

"Kurt!" I exclaimed. In the mad spectacle of the final few minutes I had forgotten his immense courage and I sagged at the loss of one of my oldest comrades and dearest friends.

"Regrettable, but that's the fortunes of war I'm afraid, we are doomed to lose our closest comrades. He went above and beyond to distract that foul demon, both of you did. I've rarely witnessed such courage. You should be proud of him and yourself."

"And Jürgen?"

"I'm afraid he too made the ultimate sacrifice."

"But what was that creature? The cat being I mean, why did it come to our aid?"

"Bastet? Ah Bastet is no creature, but an entity, a goddess you might say from another almost forgotten age. Fortunately for us, she is, if not exactly friendly, at least neutral in her feelings towards mankind but when one of her subjects is threatened she may sometimes be called upon to lend a hand," here he tickled Little Hans under the chin to the cat's evident delight.

"She didn't need much of an inducement to intervene if I'm honest.

The serpent god and his subjects are and will always remain her mortal enemies and with the right... prompting, she will readily take up the ancient feud."

"And that prompting included the Obersturmführer and Little Hans?

"Yes but they were mere vessels for her form, much more important was the altar, though altar it has not always been. That is only its current configuration, a fact which our dear Obersturmführer would have known if she'd researched her subject more thoroughly. She always was a bit of a hack, her ambition overmatching her ability. No grasp of the fundamentals you see, always looking for the shortcut, the quick and easy route to power.

"No, the altar is an artefact that has taken many forms and been known by many names down the ages. The Fangs of Set, the Dagger of Thoth and yes, even the Claws of Bastet, see?"

He held up a magnificent necklace made of a strange unearthly metal, which was burnished with what looked like jewelled cats' eyes, the rare metals forming ornate claws tipped with all manner of intricately carved hieroglyphs.

"That, that's the altar?" I asked and he nodded.

"Yes, the altar indeed, the Fangs of Set in a sparkling new and even more portable form. Many creatures, many races, have claimed it as their own down the millennia, for it is an ancient artefact of great power, great potential and great mischief. One which I'm pleased to say I will now be able to place safely beyond the reach of mortal man. That has always been my aim, right from the beginning, when I first had word of Sweet Liesel's intentions. This damn war's complicated enough without drawing any of the lesser races in, but I'm not sure your *Führer* or the Black Sun would take the same view."

"What happens now?"

"Now? Well the first order of business is to get out of here before this place sinks beneath the sands again. Milady's spell won't hold it forever and now Bastet has departed, her furry subjects won't keep the serpent men occupied for very long. I don't know about you, but I don't think we want to be here when they get back."

"Not at all."

"So let's wake her and..." Captain Seraph looked to where the Obersturmführer had fallen, but now there was no-one there.

"Well played, Sweet Liesel, well played, " said the captain. "Evidently you have more strings to your bow than I gave you credit for. Oh well, we'll meet again ... we always do, you know.

"Come, for I believe I can hear the snake men about to make their return. Give me your hand, we should be able to scale that rubble without too much difficulty and I for one will be glad for some clean air and the dawn's light upon me. We have been far too long in this nest of vipers."

So there you have it gentlemen. Naturally I do not expect you to believe my report, for if I were presented with such a tale, I would send its teller straight to the lunatic asylum, throw away the keys and good riddance. But I can assure you I am quite sane and despite its many fantastic aspects, this story is as true as these strange scars I bear, or this little kitten you see sleeping on my lap.

As for the rest? Well, with the captain's assistance we did indeed make our way out of the pyramid and commandeered one of the vehicles which the Black Sun had left behind. We drove until the ziggurats were just a fading mirage in our mirrors. Then as the true dawn began to break across the desert, we watched the complex slowly slip beneath the sands again, until nothing remained to show that they had ever been there.

We drove along in silence for a while, the captain friendly enough but thoughtful, preoccupied, perhaps contemplating the implications of our adventure. I felt many things, relief, grief, but also an immense exhaustion and as the sun established its hegemony over the sands and the heat began to rise, I must confess, my weary eyelids succumbed and I was soon asleep in the passenger seat. I awoke when your men found me and brought me here, but as for the captain? There was not a single trace of him and when I asked them about my companion, they said they had discovered me alone.

What happened to Captain Seraph I do not know, but I imagine he has his own singular path to tread and that he had left me there, so close to your lines, so that I might be discovered and brought to safety.

As for him, well perhaps he is still out there, roaming the wastes for all I know, and I, you, we, should all be glad of it. For we need men like him to protect us from both the unseen terrors that lurk at the margins of the world and the foolish, irresponsible notion that we may be able to harness them to our own selfish ends.

JOIN THE BATTLE AGAINST THE DEADLY MENACE OF THE MYTHOS!

Delve into the thrilling worlds of the Seraph Chronicles and Mon Dieu Cthulhu! and join Major Seraph and French hussar Gaston Dubois as they begin their fight against the powers of darkness!

Head over to www.john-houlihan.net and sign up for the newsletter to receive a free bonus story from either universe which reveals more about these exciting worlds.

You'll also get updates on new work including the forthcoming Keeper of the Hidden Flame, an epic new adventure in the Mon Dieu Cthulhu! series. In it Gaston Dubois reunites with Major Seraph to be inducted into a secret society who have long guarded humanity against the powers of the dark.

There's also regular freebies, giveaways and competitions and a chance to participate in the development of the forthcoming Mon Dieu Cthulhu! tabletop roleplaying game!

THE SERAPH CHRONICLES
One man defies the might of dread Cthulhu!

The Trellborg Monstrosities

It is 1943 and the war hangs on a knife edge. Set free by a leading Nazi occultist, an ancient evil stirs in the snowy fastnesses of the Norwegian border, threatening to unleash an ancient artefact which could not only alter the course of the war, but the fate of humanity itself.

Hope though endures, as a band of brave resistance fighters and a crack team of British special forces combine to plunge deep behind enemy lines to confront this ancient horror. Yet is their strange civilian adviser, the mysterious Mister Seraph, truly on the side of the angels or pursuing some dark agenda of his own? Can the fearful Trellborg terror even be defeated by mere mortal men?

"A wonderfully evocative tale of blood, bullets and ice." – David J Rodger

The Crystal Void

The year is 1810 and as Napoleon's marshals chase Wellington's expeditionary force through Spain to the lines of Torres Verdras, dashing if rather dim French Hussar Gaston Dubois is astonished to encounter the love of his life.

But the fragrant Odette is abducted before Dubois can consummate his passion by the Marquis Da Foz, a ruthless and sadistic Portuguese nobleman. The hot blooded Hussar is soon in deadly pursuit, but can he evade the Marquis' myriad traps and who is the mysterious ally, Major Seraph, who comes to his aid?

What strange horrors lurk within the shadows of the ancient Moorish fortress where Odette is held captive? Can the heroic duo foil Da Foz's dark machinations, defeat his unnatural allies, rescue Odette and prevent the opening of the dreaded Crystal Void, before it unleashes a new reign of terror on the world?

"Great story, interesting characters, lots of sword and musket action, and the potential for future stories in an underutilised setting."
– Sci-fi and Fantasy Reviewer

Tomb of the Aeons

'The sands of the desert seem as unchanging as the aeons, but they constantly shift reform and remake themselves, so that one is always looking at a frozen moment in perpetual chaos.' – Commander Siegfried

It is 1941 and as Ernst Rommel, the Desert Fox, swings his great armoured right hook to send the British Eighth Army scurrying back toward Egypt, the crew of Ingrid, a mark IV panzer pursue a lone British tank into the deep wastes, only to be ambushed and knocked out.

When they awake, Ingrid's commander Siegfried and his surviving crew begin the long weary trudge back to their own lines, but soon become lost in an unnatural sand storm which seems to blow up from nowhere. When they stumble upon a strange temple complex and find a unit of dead Black Sun SS, they are forced to penetrate deep into the heart of the unholy ziggurat and recover a lost artefact, the Fangs of Set, by their guide and fellow captive Captain Seraph. Will they defeat this charnel house's newly awoken inhabitants and can they survive the horror lurking at the very centre of this tomb of the aeons?

"Indiana Jones meets HP Lovecraft" – Monty Burnham

"The writing is excellent and the atmosphere well-maintained ... it deserves to be widely read." – Sci-fi and Fantasy Reviewer

Before the Flood

The year is 2034 and Britain is a drowning isle, after a cataclysmic wave destroyed her cities, killing millions, raising the sea level by 60 metres and changing the landscape forever.

The Flood has brought Albion to her knees and now the Devils, a race of malevolent sea creatures, haunt her coasts as the survivors retreat inland, struggling for their very existence.

Mankind learns to fear the sea and avoid the water.

Then a mysterious island surfaces off the coast of Wales, a small team of British militia under the command of the war weary veteran Sergeant Emma Stokes, is dispatched to investigate this new threat. But a chance meeting with the mysterious Major Seraph takes them on a dangerous odyssey through this drowned world, to the hidden fortress-city of Gwaelod, which seems to offer new hope in the battle against the creatures. Yet as humanity clutches on by its fingertips, who are the real enemies in this deadly flooded world?

"The shape of water was not a love story, it was a warning."
Amazon Reviewer

"A cracking story. Pick up Before The Flood and devour it, then go onto the rest of the Seraph Chronicles. You'll be in for a hell of a ride!" -
Sci-fi and Fantasy Reviewer

SCIENCE FICTION

The Constellation of Alarion and Other Stories

Best Short Fiction Nominee British Science Fiction Association 2021

Ten insightful science fiction tales from one of British sci-fi and fantasy's most intriguing authors.

John Houlihan is best known for his Cthulhu mythos and historical fantasy series, but this is his first major collection of sci-fi stories, including debut play, Bomber Command.

In Most Exalted, the hero of the seven systems now resides in retirement, but when a series of suspicious deaths rock his veterans' home, will his dubious past finally catch up with him?

In Charioteer, countries settle disputes the old fashioned way, trial by combat. As the eve of a great contest draws close, will Soola finally step out of her brother's shadow and embrace her true destiny?

In the Constellation of Alarion, a fabulous treasure lies hidden in the midst of a deadly labyrinth. Can three galaxy-hopping rogues overcome the maze's lethal traps and their own bumbling inadequacies to claim it?

Explore ten tantalising tales and take a glimpse into a beguiling sci-fi future from one of fantastic fiction's most fascinating talents.

"A masterful collection" Sci-Fi and Fantasy Reviewer

Dark Tales from the Secret War

Dark Tales is a collection of 13 stories set in Modiphius' Achtung! Cthulhu universe, a world which mixes the terrors of HP Lovecraft's Cthulhu mythos with mankind's darkest yet finest hour, the Second World War. Thirteen unhallowed stories await within its covers, which range from the wilds of the South Pacific to the dark depths of the Black Forest, to the icy wastes of Norway. Edited by John Houlihan they come from a stellar cast of writers including David J Rodger, Martin Korda, Richard Dansky and the unsettling mind of horror master Patrick Garratt.

Expanding and exploring the Achtung! Cthulhu universe in bold, new narrative ways, these are the darkest of tales from the Secret War and feature the nefarious Black Sun, Nachtwolfe and their Nazi masters and the heroic Allied forces of Section M and Majestic, as well as many thrilling standalone adventures.

Dark Tales is available from Modiphius.net

MON DIEU CTHULHU!
Swashbuckling supernatural adventure!

The Crystal Void Illustrated Version

The year is 1810 and as Napoleon's marshals chase Wellington's expeditionary force through Spain to the lines of Torres Verdras, dashing if rather dim French Hussar Gaston Dubois is astonished to encounter the love of his life.

But the fragrant Odette is abducted before Dubois can consummate his passion by the Marquis Da Foz, a ruthless and sadistic Portuguese nobleman. The hot blooded Hussar is soon in deadly pursuit, but can he evade the Marquis' myriad traps and who is the mysterious ally, Major Seraph, who comes to his aid?

What strange horrors lurk within the shadows of the ancient Moorish fortress where Odette is held captive? Can the heroic duo foil Da Foz's dark machinations, defeat his unnatural allies, rescue Odette and prevent the opening of the dreaded Crystal Void, before it unleashes a new reign of terror on the world?

"Great story, interesting characters, lots of sword and musket action, and the potential for future stories in an underutilised setting."
— Sci-fi and Fantasy Reviewer

Feast of the Dead

It is late 1810 and as autumn turns to winter, Napoleon's Armee Iberian settles down to its siege of Wellington's "accursed earthworks" at Torres Vedras. Dashing French Lieutenant, Gaston Dubois, is given his first independent command: leading a detachment of hussars those "thieves on horseback" into the Spanish interior, in search of intelligence, supplies and plunder.

After a bloody skirmish, Dubois and his men take refuge at the Monasterio de St Cloud, an ancient ruin standing at the crossroads of this war-torn land, which now serves as a field hospital to soldiers of all nations. There, he encounters the unworldly Doctor Malfeas and the beautiful but fierce Mademoiselle Brockenhurst, who seem to offer temporary respite from the horrors of war.

Yet this former house of the holy holds many strange secrets and Dubois faces fresh battles on all fronts. In his own ranks against the surly Sergeant Sacleaux, his disgraced second-in-command, and externally, by a hostile countryside where every hand is turned against him. Yet most sinister of all is the malevolent mystery which lies at the heart of the Monasterio itself, an ancient and terrible enigma which threatens both the lives and souls of all who encounter it.

Alone, deep behind enemy lines and beset on all sides, will Dubois survive his first real command and can he prevent the horrible unravelling of the mysterious feast of the dead?

"An epic, swashbuckling Napoleonic adventure expertly blended with chilling Lovecraftian horror. One of the most accomplished, entertaining and quietly chilling Horror novels that I've come across in my dive into the genre." – Sci-fi and Fantasy Reviewer

"Highly entertaining, mixing history and fantasy for great adventures ... fall in love with Dubois and his inimitable style." – Egretia.com

Shadow of the Serpent

As the year 1810 wanes, dashing hussar Lieutenant Gaston Dubois finds himself at a crossroads. Following a duel over a crime passionnel, he is banished from his beloved 13th Death's Head Hussars and dispatched in disgrace to the "Accursed" 31st Dragoons

Placed in command of the unruly Second Company in a posting far from the glory and honour he craves, Dubois faces a series of challenges in his first formal command. Can he transform his dispirited men into an effective fighting force, prove his ability to command, and escape the murderous attentions of an odious fellow officer?

But even in this forgotten corner of the war, the forces of mythos and mystery are never far away. Dubois' duel was fought against no mortal man and he is plagued by uncanny events, a countryside hostile to the French occupiers and the wrath of a fearsome guerilla bandita, La Espina, who seems determined to have his head.

Called to arms in a decisive battle against the Spanish army, can Dubois and his company perform in the heat of battle, lead them to victory and restore his reputation and his honour?